LIVE GREEN
OR DIE TRYING
An Urban Farm Mystery

YVONNE LOVEDAY

LIVE GREEN OR DIE TRYING
(An Urban Farm Mystery, Book 1)

Cover photography by Tovah Love Photography
www.tovahlovephotography.com

Published in the United States of America 2014 by Yvonne Loveday

Amazon Kindle E-book ASIN: B00LS7LNW8

Paperback ISBN: 978-09906513-0-7

*If you want to tell people the truth, make them laugh,
otherwise they'll kill you.*

—Oscar Wilde

« PROLOGUE »

SHE FLUNG HERSELF OUT into the night at the bottom of the stairs. Her breath was ragged as she skirted the Sunsphere, praying that the building shielded her from her pursuer while she decided what to do. The car. Where was the car?

She heard his heavy footfall as the stairwell door slammed open again. She hesitated for a beat, then turned toward the Amphitheater, her heart pounding. She barreled across the plaza toward the man-made lake. She had no plan. She could only run from the footsteps gaining ground behind her.

A hand grabbed her by the hair and yanked hard. She jerked back violently and went down, hitting the concrete with a sickening thud. She kicked and screamed as he dragged her the remaining distance to the water. She scrambled desperately, clawing his boots, his knees. She scratched at his arms, any exposed skin.

He cursed and pulled harder.

She screeched until her face slammed into the water. She thrashed as the flood burst into her lungs, her head exploding with lights and the sound of churning water. Her throat burned and her ears pounded as she vainly lashed out at the man behind her.

He shoved her deeper underwater. He didn't stop until she was still.

He stood knee-deep in the shallow pool mesmerized by the way her hair fanned out in a halo until the sound of approaching sirens brought him back. Panting and wet, he jumped out of the water and ran for the truck where the others waited. They peeled off in a cloud of burning rubber.

« CHAPTER 1 »

THREE MONTHS EARLIER

David means "beloved." And he was, so very much. Nobody seemed to see the taunt in the way he died. The headlines read "Local Activist Killed in Biking Accident." That was only one tiny piece of the story.

Nowhere did it say that the truck was hauling asparagus from Peru to Tennessee grocery stores. David would have scoffed at the distance the out-of-season asparagus traveled to get to Knoxville tables. He would have said nobody should be eating it anyway. It's an early spring vegetable, and it was autumn. He would have been furious that it traveled 3,200 miles as the crow flies, and God only knows how far by sea and highway, to maybe get to local tables.

That is what David would have said. His wife Emma used to spend a lot of time spinning the real headline in her head, the truth that others didn't see.

"Slow Food Activist Mowed Down by Truckload of Peruvian Asparagus."

"Zero-Carbon Advocate Killed by Carbon-Spewing Semi."

After a considerable fit of fury, David would have laughed at the irony. He would have mused that, unlike the rest of us, the poor bicyclist got the full effect of our unhealthy attitudes toward food and the environment, right up the side of the head instead of gradually with every bite we eat and every breath we take. This bicyclist who was pedaling to keep carbon emissions out of the atmosphere was squashed by a truck that got four miles to the gallon and used 120 gallons of gas a day.

These kinds of facts swim around in the heads of those left behind by the dead. Every minute detail of death is parsed and chewed over. Emma drowned daily in the twisted incongruity of David's death, particularly the last headline flashing over and over in her head.

"Supposed Faithful Husband Dies after Leaving Girlfriend's Bed."

What an obituary that would have made.

David Goode, 53, local activist, was killed in a tragic accident after leaving the home of his girlfriend and fellow activist, Molly Steed, 33. Goode leaves behind his wife Emma, 52; and two sons, Edward, 30, and Abe, 24.

Had everyone known this humiliating truth but her? David, the one true and uncompromising soul, her soul, was having an affair. Why hadn't she seen the signs? Even the question was humiliating. She only found out when an unmarked package came in the mail a month after his death. It contained a video tape. She thought it was another homegrown production, some urban farmer's homemade demonstration movie. After putting it in the VCR, it took Emma a moment to discern what was on the screen—rumpled sheets, naked flesh, and tousled dark hair. The moment of realization ripped through her raggedly. She was looking at a homemade sex tape. David and Molly laughing. David and Molly touching.

She cried out as she fumbled the tape out of the VCR. Grabbing scissors on the desk, she pulled the magnetic tape out of its case, cutting its entire length into what seemed like a mountain of shiny, brown, half-inch pieces. Consumed by grief and outrage, she swept them up in her arms and burned it all in the fire pit on the back patio. David would have disapproved of the fumes and black smoke from the burning plastic.

Emma didn't care.

These thoughts rattled round and round in her head every time she came to the garden. They made big plans for this garden. David called it the Grand Experiment. They were going to produce most of their food here and show urbanites that backyard organic farms could work. They read all the literature and toured every urban farm in the region. They practiced on a small scale with heirloom tomatoes and sweet chocolate peppers. David delighted in the fat brown peppers with the sweetest taste. She became a tomato connoisseur: Brandywines, Arkansas Travelers, Tomatillo Verde. They joyfully tended that kitchen garden and had big plans to go all out the following spring, incorporating every square-foot of their yard into food production.

And then David died. The garden lay fallow that spring. Emma tried more than once to get back to the garden. She took her hoe and shovel and dug the rich earth in the beds, but all she could think about was betrayal. With every shovelful of dirt she turned over, she felt like she was turning over more lies. She stabbed the ground with her hoe. She fell to her knees and pounded it with her fists. She sobbed and raged until, broken, she got up and went back inside.

That was the first spring. She was only glad her sons hadn't been there to watch her. Edward, their oldest, was a prosecuting attorney in Las Vegas. He was making a career out of going after the big criminals with the biggest, "baddest" connections. He moved his family to Vegas to take on a high-profile case. He was a white hat, like his father. Emma winced, but David *was* a white hat in so many ways. She resolved that Edward would never know his father's secret.

Molly Steed was only a few years older than he was. She and David worked closely on the mayor's New Visions project. Hell, Molly sat down at her dinner table and worked late nights in her living room. Never once had Emma suspected. What a fool she had been!

And Abe, sweet Abe. He was finishing up a degree in ecological agriculture at Evergreen State College in Olympia, Washington—his choice because he could create his own independent study program. He worshiped his father and was following in his footsteps as food activist and earth steward. No, her sons would never know the truth about their father. They would never have to face the stark betrayal and bottomless shame that she felt. At least she could spare them that.

Two growing seasons passed. One day Emma emerged from her home and stood surveying the backyard, her hand shielding her eyes from the sun. The daffodils were blooming. Time to put the salad greens in the ground, the old timers said. She decided to take another stab at the garden.

***

The overgrown garden beds proved too much for Emma to tackle alone. She managed to get a good amount of spinach and other greens planted in containers on the patio, but she couldn't bear to touch the yard. A quick online search brought up a long list of local landscapers. She chose the one closest to her house, Katuah Bioregion Permaculture

Design. No answer. As instructed by the answering service, she left her name, number, address, and best time for a consultation.

Too early the next morning, a 20-something man showed up on her doorstep.

"I'm Free Byrd. Everyone calls me Teepee Free. I'm here about your garden beds."

She looked him up and down curiously. He might have stepped out of a seventies documentary about hippies, except that he had a hip urban look about him. His shoulder-length brown hair was pulled back in a ponytail, but the soul patch under his lip placed him squarely in the present. A leather lace was tied around one wrist. He wore a dark wool ivy cap, jeans, and a tee shirt that read "sound tribe sector nine." His Doc Martens were scuffed and worn.

"Why do they call you Teepee Free?" Emma eased out the door and closed it behind her.

"I build teepees," he said, with a boyish grin. "That's my life work. I do landscaping on the side. The teepee business is a bit slow right now."

They walked around to the back of the house. The backyard was about an acre, and gently sloped down to meet a small creek bed.

"Wow, big yard," Free said as he surveyed the lot. Emma looked at the yard as a stranger might. Six raised beds dotted the lawn, all bursting with weeds of every description, some as tall as Emma. Not one of David's straight even rows could be deciphered from the mess of weeds and bushes.

Free walked halfway down the yard, studying the landscape. He stopped amid the garden beds and pulled a compass out of his pocket. He aligned himself to the south, standing clear of the trees and their shade.

He pointed along the creek. "You can put fruit trees there. Maybe cattails if you get any flooding. I bet you do this time of year. They're edible, you know. Or bamboo. Of course you'll want to put your compost bin here and your rain barrels there. Maybe a pyramid of 55-gallon barrels against the house."

Now Free was gesturing around the yard.

"We can probably set up a greywater system from the house to divert water down here to the garden since that creek is so nasty. First Creek, right? It's a mess. Let's put your livestock down by the creek." He paused to take a breath.

"Livestock?" Emma's eyes bulged only slightly.

"Chickens or rabbits. You're a meat eater, right? And eggs. You'll need eggs. And manure for the gardens. Maybe goats for milk. Bees, of course."

"Of course," said a bewildered Emma. "Wait. I just want these beds cleaned up."

Free scratched his sideburns, then stroked his stubbly soul patch thoughtfully. "Emma, as responsible citizens of the Earth, we have to do all we can to live in harmony with its natural cycles. We need to reinsert ourselves into the Web of Life. Besides, I work real cheap."

"How cheap?"

"Just let me pitch my teepee down in the yard and I'll work for rent. We've got a lot of work to do here. I'll even make dinner on Thursday nights. I make a mean tofu and bulgur cabbage roll."

Teepee Free agreed to start on the gardens immediately. His tools were in the back of his truck. He took pains to tell Emma it was a grease car that ran on vegetable oil.

"I have a friend at McDonald's who calls me every time the frying oil is changed," he explained. Emma was duly impressed.

Free set about his work immediately. He pulled a scythe from the back of the truck. Its sharp edges seemed to sing as they slashed through the overgrowth in the garden beds. He stooped occasionally to pull plants out by the roots.

"Raised beds are fine, but I like to put plants straight in the ground," Free said as he picked up a pile of cut weeds. "Just my opinion, of course. I like to work with the natural landscape, better to simulate nature. We could make an amazing food forest back here."

He paused to take off his shirt, wiping his face with it before he threw it aside. The spring sun was warm, and Free, obviously not a deodorant wearer, was starting to reek a little.

"You can grow a lot of food in six beds with some planning. Not all that you need, but a good chunk. Did you know that the food you buy in the grocery store can travel thousands of miles from the farm to your table? Think of the gas it takes to transport food that far. That's too much of a burden on the Earth, not to mention, homegrown food or even local food, for that matter, is fresher and better tasting."

Yes, Emma knew about food miles. She frowned at the thought. Memories of David came flooding into her mind, but she turned them off. She thought instead of her own foray into local food before the Grand Experiment. It started after reading a book about one family's herculean efforts to eat locally grown foods within a 100-mile radius of their home. *Animal, Vegetable, Miracle* had changed her life.

"I try to eat mindfully," she said as she helped move the cut weeds to the old compost pile. "My husband and I read labels and ate locally. It was a full-time job."

Teepee Free stopped swinging his scythe and looked at her. "Ah, so you are a believer. I thought as much. It looks like you had the beginnings of a nice setup here at some point. How'd it get so grown up?"

"My husband died. I pretty much quit everything." She looked down at her own scuffed yard shoes.

"I want to get back to it. Realistically, I can't grow everything I need, but this is a good start," she said. "Baby steps."

The young man snorted. "No time for baby steps, Emma. The world is in peril."

In time, she would realize that's the way Teepee Free talked. In his mind, he and his scythe were the only things standing in the way of the world's plunge into total annihilation. Maybe he was right, she thought.

When they stopped for lunch (Free brought his own sandwich of organic tomato, alfalfa sprouts, and soy mayonnaise on whole wheat bread packed in a reusable container), he asked for paper and a pen so he could sketch out his proposed improvements to Emma's backyard.

True to his word, it was all right there on paper—the gardens, the fruit trees, the compost bin, and the rest. "We could build tilapia tanks by the back porch." Free had sketched tall, conical tanks full of fish.

"Free, I can't afford tilapia tanks. I need to tackle this project in phases."

"That's okay, we'll get a grant. It'll be a demonstration house. And actually, it would be a good idea to start a blog documenting our progress. It could help the process." Free talked on about his dream of free food for the people, and tilapia tanks and apple trees in the middle of downtown. He wanted to create a hydroponic farm in an old warehouse right on Market Square, the heart of the revitalized city. He envisioned an organic "factory farm" to supply vegetables to restaurants on the Square and people who lived downtown. It would be a model for other urban farmers. Better yet, he could set up his farming operation and start a solar power business in the Sunsphere, the city's premier landmark.

"Wouldn't that be a bad ass location, and a killer statement?" he asked. "Solar power coming from the Sunsphere!"

"Well, it sure would be nice to find a use for the Sunsphere. It has pretty much sat empty since the World's Fair in '82," Emma replied.

All Emma could think of was trekking solar panels and other gear up and down the 266-foot, steel-truss base to the golden, orb-shaped sphere of offices at the top, but in spite of that, she was swept up by his vision. It made poetic sense. And though it seemed a bit quixotic by her standards, Free was the person who could possibly pull it off. He wasn't all vision. He seemed like a hard worker. Maybe he just needed help.

By the end of the conversation, she had agreed to help Free with his projects. Work and a tofu dinner in exchange for rent, in exchange for grant writing in exchange for vegetables and tilapia. The bartering was flying around so fast and furious that Emma wasn't sure who owed what to whom, but if anyone could keep track of it all, it was Free.

It was easy to trust this young man. He was nothing if not sincere. His grasp of ecology and sustainable gardening practices was impressive. His earnestness was refreshing.

Emma later wondered why she let the young man into her life so easily. Perhaps it was his seeming innocence and visionary ecological views, a beguiling combination. The young man had faith in the world's ability to change, an uncommon trait among kids his age. Maybe it was because her two sons were grown and living far away. She saw Free as a kindred spirit. She envied his nomadic lifestyle. There was a time in her life when she jumped in her truck and hit the roads for parts unknown. She missed those days. Free was full of the youthful exuberance that she once felt but had lost after the long years of babies and work and too many bills.

***

Free liked Emma the second he laid eyes on her. It wasn't sexual attraction. It was the feeling you get when you meet a member of your spirit tribe. Even with a three-decade age difference, they met on a level that most people never seem to reach. It wasn't often that he could just start spouting his vision for the community and not have to explain everything he meant, or why it was a good idea, or why the prevailing paradigm was bad. Emma got it. She got him.

Emma had set a fast pace when they started weeding her gardens. She was healthy, almost athletic, and pretty in an unpretentious way, almost as an afterthought. Most women her age had long since cut their hair, but hers hung over her shoulder in a long white braid. He figured she was about the same age as his mother, so that white hair was definitely premature. Her green eyes were wise and her smile was kind, but she seemed so very, very sad.

"So where are you from, Free?" They worked side by side throughout the afternoon.

"Arcata, California, originally. I was raised off the grid in a commune."

"Wow. There's a story there, I bet."

Was there ever. Free told Emma he was the only son of two hippies, suckled on ideas of right livelihood and visions for an alternative world. As a child, he spent a lot of time in the woods and ran with the goats and dogs when he wasn't being home-schooled by a laid-back lady named Bluejay. He lived in an old travel trailer on 100 acres with his parents, Bard and Star—not their given names—and several other families who came and went over the years. Some lived in tents. Some lived in teepees or other non-permanent structures like his family's trailer. Bard was a retired sociology professor. Star was a nurse who mostly ran free clinics. They grew a lot of their own food and cooked outside. Any electricity they used came from the solar panels that

Bard set up like wings on the sides of their trailer. Oh, and pedal power. The use of small appliances was contingent on the amount of muscle exerted.

"So you learned early to distrust authority and disregard convention," Emma said.

"Absolutely. And I learned how long I had to pedal to blend my smoothie in a converted 12-volt blender."

"How long?"

"Not as long as you'd think if you don't use ice."

"Do you live in a teepee by choice?"

"I'd rather live in my teepee than anywhere else."

"What do you do when it gets cold?"

"I rely on the kindness of strangers."

He explained that he used public buildings for amenities like running water, electricity, and free wireless for his computer. He drove his 1994 Ford F350 truck far more than he felt he should, but since it ran on vegetable oil, he didn't feel too guilty.

"In a perfect world, I could walk and bike everywhere I needed to go. Unfortunately, Knoxville is not the friendliest town for bikers. And everything is so spread out. Then there's the issue of my tools. I drive as little as possible because I can't always get a lot of used French-fry oil."

He had a friend who made the gas-to-vegetable oil conversions.

"Just let me know when you're ready to convert your car and I'll hook you up."

Apparently, it wasn't hard if you drove the right kind of car (diesel) and knew a gearhead who was into those kinds of things. Plus, one needed a reliable used vegetable oil hookup. Fortunately he had one. This seemed to salve his conscience at a time when Peak Oil—the point when global oil production reaches its maximum rate and starts a steady decline—was of major consequence.

They worked until dinner time and made arrangements to reconvene in the garden the next day. Free had had a good day. Tonight he would get started on that blog. Surely the planets had aligned and his spirit guides were on duty the day he met Emma. Her backyard was a blank slate. With his connections and her own green aspirations, together they could make an alternative mecca out of this property, an oasis of hope and awareness in a culture on the skids.

KNOXTOPIA
Plant a Garden. Change the World.

Welcome to the first post of our new blog, Knoxtopia. We are two people growing an urban farm in Knoxville, Tennessee. Emma owns the place. I'm Teepee Free, the bartered hand. Let me start our adventure with this truism:

URBAN FARMING IS THE MOST IMPORTANT MOVEMENT OF OUR TIME.

Everyone eats. The simple act of planting a garden instead of buying from giant supermarket chains changes the debate on issues like health, economics, and politics. By doing so, we take back control over what goes into our food and, hence, our bodies. We create the world we want to live in—one free from poisons, unfair practices, and unscrupulous companies and politics.

Who knew a tomato plant wielded that much power?

By planting an organic garden, we unplug from oil. We reject oil-based fertilizers and insecticides. We no longer need all that plastic packaging. Our food isn't trucked in gas-guzzling planes, trucks, and trains.

Best of all, we honor our bodies with food free from poison and scary bio-engineered organisms. Think about this: If we are what we eat, we are drenching ourselves in pesticides and unnatural organisms when we eat heavily fertilized plants from seeds bio-engineered to kill pests. No thanks!

All this, PLUS our homegrown food is uber-healthy, juicy, and delicious. And did I mention that through organic practices we are healing our imperiled Mother Earth? There's no down side to this.

So friends, here we will document Emma's journey to self-sufficiency in the city. Come with us as we transform Emma's ordinary city home into a farm oasis only 10 houses down from a major thoroughfare. We are building a real-life working model for sustainable agriculture and eco-living in a major metropolis. We aren't the first to do this. Documenting our labors here will ensure we aren't the last. Expect to learn about our adventures in organic farming, city farm animals, permaculture, alternative energy, water and waste management, and more.

Bookmark our blog and come back often. We'll keep you posted.

2 Comments

GreenbyNature said ...

Fantastic! I look forward to many more posts.

AnnieSpeaks said ...

Welcome to the world of blogging! Please join me at Annie_Speaks, a blog about Knoxville night life!

« CHAPTER 2 »

EMMA SIPPED HER COFFEE as she stared out the kitchen window toward Free's teepee. Nearly 20 feet tall, the top half of the canvas was painted cobalt blue. White constellations were painted all around it, like the night sky. It was a beautiful thing to behold.

More than two weeks had passed since Free had come on the scene, and things were working out nicely. He worked his landscaping jobs around Emma's yard projects. That worked out because she had to work, too. She was a freelance writer and editor. David left her enough for bills and necessities. Everything else came from what work she could scrape up for herself.

Free usually was gone by early evening. Emma didn't know where he went. She didn't ask, but he was back by morning. Sometimes he regaled her while they worked with tales of this environmental defense meeting or that home cheese-making demonstration at the food co-op. Free got around in the alternative underground.

Today she was heading downtown to the Farmer's Market for vegetable seeds and plants, and depending on what she found there, maybe to a nearby nursery. The first of May was the grand opening of the Farmer's Market and a traditional planting day for the region. It was tempting to plant before then, especially as the days grew warmer. Old timers warned against it, though, except of course for early greens and root crops. April was a dangerous month for unexpected frosts in the Tennessee Valley. In fact, many long-time farmers held off until Mother's Day.

She and Free had weeded and added compost to most of the raised beds. Free found composted manure at the Knoxville Zoo. They built a new compost bin by the garden. Already she was filling it with spent coffee grounds, kitchen scraps, and yard waste. They were weeding and pulling up scrubby vegetation along the creek to make room for edible landscaping like apple and Asian pear trees. Free was nearly finished with a chicken coop.

Before her shopping trip, though, she needed to get some work done. Working from home was its own challenge. Too many distractions pulled at her as she edited other people's manuscripts. However, business was good. She couldn't complain. She sighed as she settled into the chair at her desk. She was only a few pages into her manuscript when the phone rang.

"Goode Editing Service. Emma speaking."

"Em, you should call your business *Great* Editing Service." It was Vergie Dell, Emma's next-door neighbor. And that joke was old, seeing as how Vergie told it every time she called. In fact, if she had a nickel for every time Vergie Dell called to harass her over something, she would be very rich indeed.

"Hello, Vergie. How are you today?"

"Emma Lee, what *is* that in your backyard?"

"Are you just noticing it, Vergie? It's been there for two weeks."

"I've been off to a summer tent revival in Johnson City," Vergie drawled. "Some forty souls came to the Lord. It was a miracle."

"Hmm." Emma distractedly replaced the word *that* with *who* in the manuscript on the computer screen. It's *who* when it comes after a person and *that* when it comes after a thing, she thought crossly.

"So, what's going on? I didn't even notice 'til you chopped down that bush by the hickory tree."

"Well, Vergie, a young man is helping me do some yard work. He stays in the teepee."

"Who is he?"

"His name is Teepee Free."

"Toilet paper? Why's he named after toilet paper?"

"No, *teepee*. The cone-shaped tent, not toilet paper."

"What's he do?

"He's a landscaper."

"Since when do landscapers move in with you? What's going on? I think that's against city code anyway, having that tent down there like that."

"It's temporary, and he's a guest, so I think we're okay." Irritation was growing in Emma's voice.

"Emma Lee, is that *proper*?" The word was loaded with implication. "A widow like you, living alone for all this time, with a *man* in her backyard? *Watch and pray, that ye enter not into temptation.*"

"Vergie! He's younger than my youngest son!"

"Exactly. And just what would Abe think?"

"Abe would think, 'Awesome, now I don't have to feel guilty for not being there to help mom with the yard work.' Anyway, he reminds me a little of Abe."

"I'm just saying, Emma Lee. *The spirit indeed is willing, but the flesh is weak.*"

"Okay, that's just sick. I've got to get back to work. Thanks for your concern, Vergie."

"I'll keep my eye on him, Emma Lee." She hung up.

***

The Farmer's Market was one of David's favorite haunts. Every Wednesday during the growing season he walked down to Market Square from the mayor's office and met Emma for lunch. They then leisurely ambled from booth to booth while he carefully selected local produce for the week. By the time he got home that night, he had planned a feast around his in-season purchases. He served each Wednesday night meal with great fanfare.

This was the first time Emma had been back to the Market since David died. David liked that the crowds were smaller on Wednesday. He could linger over the tables and chat with the farmers. A wave of emotion hit her as she rounded the corner from the parking garage. How many of them knew about David's infidelity? How many of them secretly pitied her? This was their place, but mostly it was David's place. He haunted it still. Maybe this was a mistake. She paused as she struggled to gain control of her emotions. In a surge of panic, she considered running back to the car.

"Keep it together, Goode," she said under her breath. She squared her shoulders, crossed the plaza, and stepped up to the first booth. Tables were arranged in rows down the length of the pedestrian-only city block. Swallowing her emotion, Emma browsed the booths until she found the greenhouse vendor.

"Emma! Long time, no see!" Janet sat behind a booth filled with luscious, potted, green plants. This year she had an excellent variety of native plants and seeds.

"Hello, Janet. It's good to see you again." Emma fumbled with the list she and Free had penned the night before. "I'm firing up the backyard garden after a little hiatus. I have a long list."

"Great news! I've missed you," Janet said as she looked over the list and helped Emma make her choices.

Peppers. Basil. Cilantro. Lots and lots of tomatoes to eat fresh and for canning. Okra. Squash. Cucumbers. It was a good thing she'd remembered her portable grocery cart.

She made her way down the open-air aisles, speaking briefly to the regular farmers. Enough time had passed that they didn't linger over condolences about David. Feeling relieved, she bought fresh asparagus, lettuce, and early peas. She bought cabbage with Free's tofu cabbage rolls in mind. Tomorrow was his night to cook. She bought fingerling potatoes, baby spinach, and a fresh loaf of homemade whole wheat bread. Before long she found herself at Krutch Park, on the south side of the Square.

A perfect place for tilapia tanks and apple trees, Emma thought. She laughed to herself as she realized Free's dreams were invading her own. She lingered at the park while eating a tamale from one of the food trucks and imagining the food forest of Krutch Park. Making the circuit back to the north end of the mall, she stopped to look at a large FOR LEASE sign on a storefront between the Indian restaurant and smoothie stand. Nearly half of the 20 or so businesses here on Market Square were restaurants, not to mention several just a block away on Gay Street. In that moment, Emma realized an organic, hydroponic warehouse farm was not a pipe dream. It was a very real opportunity and a sound business idea. Emma scribbled down the phone number, determined to get started on the grant idea right away.

***

She came home that afternoon to a note on the door.

Can't work tonight. Going to a gathering in Seymour. —F

"Just as well," Emma muttered to herself. "I've got a deadline."

It wasn't long before Emma was belly up to the computer, editing away. She stopped at dinnertime to steam the fresh asparagus and made a quick spinach quiche. *Heaven*, she thought. She ate at the computer, allowing herself one small glass of wine with dinner since she was still working. After eating her fill, she was back at work. If she hurried through the rest of this document tonight, she could begin research for Free's grant tomorrow.

KNOXTOPIA
Plant a Garden. Change the World.

Tomatoes as a Radical Act

Today Emma went to the Farmer's Market in downtown Knoxville in search of locally grown organic vegetable seedlings. She found tomatoes, and lots of them. One booth was overrun with organic heirloom tomato plants—just what we wanted.

Here's what she got, all are organic heirlooms well suited to our region:

For canning, she brought home six Amish Paste plants. This variety is a good producer with great canning properties. Then she bought one each of black and yellow Brandywines, which are rated high for flavor. She picked up a couple of Arkansas Travelers for their drought resistant qualities. I want to compare plants with different qualities to see what really grows well here, and what tastes the best. Next, she bought two Sophie's Choice because they are extra early, and it's hard to wait on the first tomatoes of the season.

That's a dozen tomato plants! But she didn't stop there. Four Red Cherry tomato plants completed our tomato madness, because who can live without cherry tomatoes? In the spring, gardeners are cursed with the disease of thinking too big. It comes from months of salivating over seed catalogs, just itching for the first days of planting. Eating greenhouse tomatoes at the end of the winter after home-canned tomatoes are gone makes one absolutely ravenous for a homegrown tomato by spring. So we overdo it.

Peppers! California Wonder (4 plants) and Czechoslovakian Black (2). Chinese Five-Color (1) and Fish Pepper (2). We are planning to can lots of chow chow relish and salsa, so tomatoes and peppers, here we come.

She also bought Clemson Spineless okra plants, and White Wonder and Lemon cucumber plants (all heirlooms). After picking up marigold seeds for pest management and a few herbs—basil, cilantro, dill, oregano, and parsley—she called it a day. In a few days we'll be planting these babies and assessing our further needs and space. We know we're planting berries as well.

If you aren't lucky enough to have heirloom plants and seeds at your Farmer's Market, check out these companies:

Southern Exposure Seed Exchange
(highly recommended if you live in the South)

Baker Creek Heirloom Seed Company

Seed Savers Exchange

Johnny's Seeds

Friends, I can't stress enough the importance of heirloom plants over hybrids and GMOs. Please research your seed sources! Monsanto is secretly buying up heirloom companies.

Here are a few definitions for you:

Heirloom plants are grown from seeds that have been around for centuries (in many cases). They are the true variety. Their seeds can be harvested for future crops and will produce true. Get organic heirloom plants and seeds whenever you can.

Hybrid plants have been cross-pollinated to create plants with "better" qualities. By combining the best attributes of two plants, they might grow faster or produce bigger fruit. The problem with hybrids is that they are one-hit wonders. They won't reproduce true in second and later generations. Therefore you can't save the seeds and must purchase more seeds every season. Sustainable farming depends on seed saving from season to season.

Unlike hybrid seeds, **GMO** plants are not created using natural, low-tech methods like cross-pollination. GMO seed varieties are created in a lab using high-tech and sophisticated techniques like gene-splicing. This process doesn't just cross plants, it crosses different biological kingdoms. For example, Monsanto has crossed genetic material from bacteria known as Bt (Bacillus thuringiensis) with corn. The goal was to create a pest-resistant plant. This means that any pests attempting to eat the corn plant will die since the pesticide is part of every cell of the plant. It also means you are eating pesticides when you ingest it. (Don't get me started, but Bt Corn is itself registered as a pesticide with the EPA).

So, why heirloom? Hybrid seeds aren't particularly bad except for this: Our food supply is profoundly at risk. We've lost 93 percent of our plant biodiversity to hybridized, genetically modified, industrial monocultures. The loss of genetic seed diversity facing us today may lead to a catastrophe far beyond our imagining. Think Irish potato famine, but global. We urban homesteaders can do our part by growing heirlooms.

Grow your own organic food free from genetic modification and toxic chemicals! Not only does it taste better, but it is better for you—for all of us.

4 Comments

GreenbyNature said ...

Well said! Another great post.

PearlyMussel said ...

Great blog. Don't forget the connection between religion and agribusiness/farm factories. It is the underlying assumption that "man has dominion" that causes these gross infractions against nature.

VergieD said ...

Then God said, "Let Us make man in Our image, according to Our likeness; and let them rule over the fish of the sea and over the birds of the sky and over the cattle and over all the earth, and over every creeping thing that creeps on the earth.

AnnieSpeaks said ...

Wonderful post! Join me at Annie_Speaks, a blog for and about Knoxville night life.

« CHAPTER 3 »

PEARLY MUSSEL, A.K.A. Tiffany Sims, was looking forward to tonight's pagan gathering. May Day, or Beltane as the pagans called it, was her favorite ritual. She planned to dance the hell out of that maypole. Well, pagans didn't believe in hell, but she was going to dance her behind off, all the same. She also planned to drink copious amounts of May wine, salute the sun gods, and partake in a bawdy greenwood marriage. That was when you picked a partner for tonight only, according to pagan custom. Pearly really liked paganism. It was liberating.

She angled her aging Honda sedan into an open space among a dozen other cars at the farmhouse yard in Seymour, a bit south of Knoxville. Folks were gathering on the porch of the old clapboard house. Getting out of the car, she carefully donned her flowery chaplet atop her waist length blonde hair, arranging the long ribbons just so down her back. She felt just like a fairy princess in her filmy gauze skirt, camisole top, and bare feet. Her heart beat faster to the primitive sound of drums already floating from behind the house. Celebration was in the air. The bells on her ankle bracelet tinkled softly as she headed for the backyard.

A scene from fantasy greeted her as she stepped through the garden gate. Twenty or so people mingled around a table of refreshments. Many of the party-goers were dressed as fantasy creatures—fairies and Pucks and dragons. Some wore ritual garb and carried ornate staffs. A few others were wearing street clothes.

Pearly headed for the punch bowl in the middle of a long table weighed down by fruits and breads and other foods. The May bowl looked splendid with sprigs of sweet woodruff and orange wedges floating in it. She could smell the alcohol from across the yard.

"Come here often?" Pearly looked up into the eyes of a handsome man with the biggest blue eyes she had ever seen. "Okay, that was a lame line, but I couldn't resist," he said. "My name is Free."

"Most every year about this time. Hello, Free. I'm Pearly." Her voice had a natural breathlessness to it. It was ethereal, really, and dead sexy—like a New Age-y Marilyn Monroe.

Free raised one eyebrow. "Given name or—"

"Chosen," Pearly finished for him. "I took the name to honor a Tennessee endangered species of mussels, the Pearly Mussel."

Free nodded in appreciation. "They call me Teepee Free because I build teepees."

It was Pearly's turn to nod appreciatively. The night was looking up already. She dipped the ladle in the punch bowl and poured herself a cup of May wine. She took a sip, then looked up at Free flirtatiously.

"Where have I heard that name? Hey, do you write a blog? I just stumbled on it today. I use BlogFinds to keep up with all the local ones."

"Yes, that's me." Emboldened, Free continued, "This is my first time to this kind of thing so maybe you can show me around. I don't know anyone. I just read an ad in the Community section of *Metro Gnome*."

"Right on. Maybe you've seen my ad. I do reiki healing and intuitive readings."

Free shook his head. "No, but I'll look for it next week." He flashed a big smile.

"Well," Pearly drew out the word. "Where to start? Beltane is an ancient celebration of the fertilization of the earth at springtime. The maypole represents the male energy. The wreath represents the female energy. As we dance, we braid the ribbons around the pole, and the wreath descends down the pole. It's a metaphor."

"For sex?" Free liked that idea.

Pearly lowered her eyes. "Yes. We call up the fertilizing energies of the earth for the crops, but also for our lives. You know, for our prosperity and health and all the good things we want to will into our lives. We honor the god and goddess with our dance."

They looked into each other's eyes. Pearly knew that she was about to will Free into her life.

"So are you a witch? Are you in a coven?"

Pearly broke eye contact with Free to look out over the crowd. "I like to say I'm witchy. Mostly I'm into earth spirituality. I'm not nearly as serious about it as some of these other folks. I read tarot cards and dabble in astrology, but some of these people are walking encyclopedias. It's a real serious religion to them. Don't get me wrong, I'm serious about my spirituality, but I prefer drum circles to study groups. I like to call myself an eclectic witch."

"Ah." Free served himself some punch and pointed to the priest. "Who is he?"

"That's Spyder. This is his place. He's an American Traditional Witch, and his group, Green Man Grove, hosts the maypole every year." Pearly pointed to a matronly woman in a green flowing dress talking animatedly to the people around her. Her long gray hair was parted in the middle and she wore a silver diadem. A silver rope was tied around her ample middle. "That's Night Crow. She's British Traditional, the third-degree high priestess of a coven called Crow Coven. She and Spyder don't get along very well and have been at the center of a lot of witch wars around here. But all the groups get together at the major sabbats and try to get along."

"Witch Wars? British Traditional? What's that?" Free frowned. There was a lot more to this than he had expected. He envisioned the scene out of Disney's *Sword in the Stone* where the wizard chased Mad Madame Mim.

Pearly took a deep breath. "Long story, and mainly why I only show up on holy days. British Traditional Witchcraft has a lineage, though its length is highly debatable. And it's secret, like Masons. American Traditional Witchcraft grew up here in America in the sixties and seventies. It's a little more freewheeling. Hence, the witch wars. That's the short version."

"No, the short version would be to simply say they are rival groups." Free smiled charmingly. He liked this girl.

"Pagans are just like everybody else. They have their factions and arguments. I try to stay away from all those labels."

"What's your label?"

"I've been called a Fluffy Bunny because I believe in love and light, but I don't see anything wrong with that. They say that like it's a bad thing. I call myself an Earth Warrior. One guy called me a Party Pagan the other day."

"Do you like to party?"

"Very much." Pearly's laugh was low and sensual. Just as Free stepped in closer to her, a voice called out over the crowd. "Gather 'round!" Spyder stood by the maypole, arms held out expansively. "Hear ye! Hear ye! Be it known that the Grand Sabbat of Beltane is about to begin!"

A line of drummers, mostly male, stood by a freshly dug post hole in the ground. Several more men made a great fanfare of carrying a heavy, 12-foot pole trailing red and white ribbons across the yard and hoisting it upright into the hole. They stamped the earth around the pole to secure it in the ground. The women in the group cheered them on, clapping and chanting loudly. A cheer arose from the crowd, and the drummers went wild when the giant phallic symbol was fully erected.

A few party goers came forward and spaced the ribbons equidistantly around the pole. With broom handles they placed a large wildflower wreath on top of the pole, balanced by the taut ribbons. Spyder stepped up to consecrate the maypole, which, in Free's opinion, went on a little too long.

"To the dance!" shouted Spyder after the blessing. The crowd cheered and moved forward.

Free and Pearly left their cups on the table and hurried toward the maypole. As Free passed the woman called Crow, he saw her roll her eyes. A woman next to her hissed under her breath, "He's not going to cast a circle or even call sacred space?" He reached for Pearly's hand so they wouldn't get separated. He didn't plan on losing track of her.

Spyder gave them dance instructions as he and others positioned them male, then female around the pole. Night Crow and a few others chose not to dance, Free noticed. He picked up the end of a red ribbon and faced Pearly, who held a white ribbon. They pulled the ribbons as far out as they would go. Celtic music blared out of a speaker system as they danced in opposite directions around the pole, alternately ducking under the ribbons of the approaching dancers and holding their ribbons high to let the next dancer under.

Breathless and smiling, every time Pearly passed Free, she gave him a peck on the cheek. Yes, he was the one, her greenwood husband. They danced until the ribbons were braided as far down the pole as they could manage. By the end, they were bumping into each other and struggling to raise their ribbons over and under each other. They all laughed and hooted and finally called it finished. The wreath had fallen low. Spyder and a laughing woman stepped up to tie the ribbons off.

"Drink! Make merry!" Spyder called out as he shooed everyone to the table. Pearly and Free clasped hands and headed back to the punch bowl, smiling delightedly at each other.

*****

It was well after midnight when Emma looked up from her work again.

Save. Quit. Shut Down.

She closed the laptop and carried her dishes to the sink, pouring one more glass of wine before bed. The only light in the kitchen came from the accent lighting under the cabinet.

"A toast to one more finished manuscript and a little more money in the bank," she said out loud. She toasted the air and took a sip.

A movement in the backyard caught her attention. She squinted through the window. A girl was dancing in the scant moonlight. She was topless, and her long skirt twirled around her shapely legs as she pirouetted across the lower yard. Emma's gaze was transfixed at the sight.

She blinked.

Still there.

She looked at the wine glass in her hand, then back to the window. She squinted harder. Yep, that's a real girl.

Momentarily mesmerized by the dance, Emma jumped when Free rocketed out of his teepee, completely nude except for his ivy cap. He chased the girl across the yard, leaping and skipping. The girl laughed and ducked out of his way. They pranced and dodged the raised beds for a couple of minutes before Free caught her and hustled her giggling into the teepee.

Emma blinked again.

Well.

She finished her wine in one big gulp and headed for bed.

***

The next morning the doorbell rang almost as soon as Emma got out of bed.

"Emma Lee. Hello, honey." Vergie smoothed her waist-length hair and adjusted her too-large, plastic-rimmed glasses. She was wearing a calf-length jean skirt with a button-down, red-gingham top and white canvas tennis shoes. A white tri-cornered bandana was tied neatly to her head. Though she was a good twelve years younger than Emma, you couldn't tell by looking at her. "How are you today?"

"I'm fine. What brings you so early?"

"Can't I even come in?" Vergie moved as if to step into the house. Strategically, Emma partially closed the door, leaving an opening just wide enough to stand in.

"I don't mean to be inhospitable, Vergie, but I just got up. I'm not dressed and I haven't had coffee. What can I do for you?"

"I told you, I'm keeping my eyes on him." She gestured toward the backyard with her eyes. "And let me tell you," she said in a stage whisper, "they was going at it like bunnies last night in your backyard. I bet they did it three or four times."

"Vergie! How could you spy on them like that?" Emma was shocked. Sure, she noticed them back there, but she didn't peek into Free's teepee for the show.

"Honey, they was doing it right in your garden beds. I got a good look because I used Jay's night-vision goggles. *Blessed are those servants, whom the lord when he cometh shall find watching.*"

Speechless, Emma stared at her neighbor. Jay was Vergie's husband, a trucker who was gone half the time. He must be gone now because she rarely heard from Vergie when he was in town. She tried to shut the door, but Vergie's hand shot up to hold it open.

"Wait, Emma Lee! I wanted to invite you to church tonight. Reverend Floyd is giving a talk on 'The Whore of Babylon: How to Resist Temptation in a Corrupt World.' Since you have one in your backya—"

Emma closed the door and headed for the coffeepot.

A couple of hours later, Emma heard Free enter through the back door.

"Emma? You home?"

She walked into the kitchen to find him pouring coffee.

"Yes, I am. Is your company gone?"

Free smiled. "For now. Ready to get started out back?"

The morning was spent preparing the garden beds for planting. Dig. Haul. Spread. The motions of transferring the compost from the composting drum to the garden beds slowed the chatter in Emma's brain. It stopped the self-incrimination, the shame. All she could think about was the muscular strain of digging. The heft of the shovel. The weight of the rich compost. The unsteady wobble of the wheelbarrow as she angled it toward the garden. Once she found a physical rhythm, thoughts of a different nature filtered into her conscious mind.

For many months David's ghost had saturated the backyard in those wild weeds. Every time she stepped back there, the weeds touched her, tugged at her, called to her to remember. *You failed*, they seemed to say. *David never loved you. Your life was a lie.*

Cutting them back with Free's help made her feel newer, less entangled in that past. They had to dig deep for some of those roots, but the hard work was cathartic for Emma. David's presence was being exorcised, and she and Free faced a new day.

Slowly, tentatively, Emma let herself think about the goals she once shared with David. They wanted an urban homestead. She was careful to rephrase her intent. *I want an urban homestead.* David had seemed an unstoppable force when it came to changing the prevailing paradigm. Slowly, consciously she unraveled her memories of David from the principles they shared.

The Victory Garden of times past was making a comeback in the city. Some urban gardeners took it a step further. How much of our food can come from our lawns? Urban farm experiments flourished. In the past cheap oil once made transferring food all over the world an affordable enterprise. Recent soaring oil prices had caused a collapse in the system. Now that food prices were rising beyond the comfort zone for many, the issue of food quality was gaining ground.

David was leading the pack in his professional and private life. He founded Knoxville New Visions, which spearheaded community gardens and edible landscaping in the city. Through grants, David provided home composters, rain barrels, and seeds at cost for residents who wanted to garden. He was the "go to" man for the urban green scene. The mayor was so impressed with the organization that he moved it lock, stock, and barrel under his jurisdiction in the City-County Building. David walked his talk. He biked or took public transportation. He was creating his own urban farmstead. He was a community organizer and advocate for the underdog.

These were Emma's dreams too. That's why they were perfectly suited for another, or so she thought. Shame and guilt were her partners now. Her therapist had called it betrayal trauma. She said Emma had transferred guilt from David to herself. These were just words to Emma. For the life of her, she couldn't make them mean anything. Funny how the mind works. She would rather not think about it.

"By shutting down every thought of David, you've cut off many vital parts of yourself," Dr. Fairbanks had said. "Yes, urban gardening was David's pet project, but it's your pet project too. When you put that garden back together without David, you will be putting yourself back together."

She shoveled more compost.

She knew she had thrown the proverbial baby out with the bathwater. By denying all thought of David, she was denying herself. By closing out David's dreams, she had closed out her own. She had isolated herself in the process. But in this city, community organizers and activists were like a roving tribe. They moved from one issue to the next. The campaigns were different, but the people were the same. There was no dearth of peace and social justice projects, but the same few people with long memories headed them all. When they saw her, they remembered David. Emma was trying so hard to forget him. Funny, then, how thoughts of him invaded every waking moment.

But this, this she could do. Shovel. Move earth with a simple tool. The earth, this ground, was constant. It would not betray her if she tended it lovingly. This was real. It made the rest seem almost inconsequential.

Every day in the backyard felt like a new day as Emma cleared out the weeds and made her own garden plans. David's proposed lettuce bed became Emma's green bean plot. David's tomato bed was converted to melons, and Emma's tomatoes were planted in containers around the patio and in homemade upside-down planters. She was reclaiming the yard, and with it, her sense of self.

***

That afternoon Free carried the flats of plants Emma bought at Market to the beds. This was the fun part of all the work, getting the plants and seeds in the ground. Emma didn't mention her voyeuristic adventure the night before. She was a little too embarrassed to bring it up.

They worked companionably.

"Look what I've got here." Free pulled seed packets from his pocket. "Marigolds and nasturtiums. They'll keep bugs away if we plant them alongside the vegetables. Really, we should plant seedlings. Seeds take a while to germinate, but let's do it anyway." Free tore one of the packets open and knelt to plant them. "Live dangerously."

Emma poked green bean seeds into the rich earth on either side of the lattice of twine they had strung earlier that morning. Soon the delicate tendrils would reach up from the ground and curlicue around it in their attempt to reach the sun.

"Okay," she said, smoothing dirt over the indentations. "An old-timer at the market yesterday told me that the average last frost locally was around Mother's Day. Another one told me we could direct seed radishes, beets, onions, and garden greens when the daffodils bloom. Next year we'll have a huge early spring garden."

Free nodded as tucked the seeds into the bed. "Isn't it wild how we've lost that kind of knowledge? As humans living on the earth, we should know that. And to think we've lost it in just two generations." He sat back on his heels and gazed off across the yard. "People who follow the earth religions mark May first as planting time. They fertilized the fields by having sex in them."

Emma blushed and looked away. "Oh."

"And that's exactly what they did in your yard last night," Vergie said loudly as she rounded the corner of the house. "I saw them."

Free looked from Vergie to Emma. He grinned at Emma. "My little gift to your garden," he said.

"What do you *mean* having relations out in the open like that like ... like ... *animals*?" Vergie was getting worked up.

"Free, meet my neighbor Vergie. Vergie, Free."

They both looked at Emma for half a second before their eyes shot back to each other. "Vergie, nice to meet you," said Free cautiously, never taking his eyes off her.

"And this tent of yours," Vergie continued. "You're breaking city code. I looked it up on the Internet." Her eyes narrowed as she looked at Free's teepee. "Wait. What's that? A pentagram? A *pentagram*?"

Emma followed Vergie's gaze and, sure enough, an obviously homemade wreath of honeysuckle hung in the teepee door. A five-pointed star made of twigs was worked into the circle. She had to admit, it looked a little *Blair Witch*. Eyebrows raised, Emma looked at Free. Vergie's shock didn't seem to faze him.

"It's an ancient symbol denoting the four elements encircled by spirit. My friend made it last night," Free began.

"It's the sign of the Devil!" Vergie's face blanched in sickening realization. "Witches! You're witches!"

"Pagan is a more apt term," Free said. "And I'm not, really, though I sympathize with their beliefs."

"Witches!" Vergie's voice got a little louder as she recovered from the shock. "*Suffer not a witch to live*, Exodus 22:18."

"Really, Vergie. Calm down." Emma moved around the garden bed and reached to pat Vergie's arm. "It's okay. Let's talk about it."

Vergie jerked her arm away and took a step back, looking frantically from Emma to Free. "Emma Lee, I don't know what you've got yourself into, but you better shun these people now. Your immortal soul is in danger." She turned and ran back the way she had come.

"She's intense," said Free.

"Hysterical, more like," Emma said, as she watched Vergie's retreat in disbelief.

"Can the witch come to dinner tonight?" asked Free.

"Sure."

They worked until dinner time. As Free headed around to his truck with his tools, Emma looked up to see Vergie staring after him with a pair of binoculars from her upstairs window.

***

Free was still assembling cabbage rolls in the kitchen when the doorbell rang. Emma opened the door to a beautiful young lady who looked nothing like Emma's idea of a witch. Not to mention, she was fully clothed.

"Welcome to my home. I'm Emma Lee Goode." Emma extended her hand.

"I'm Pearly Mussel. Nice to meet you." The bells on Pearly's bracelets tinkled as they shook hands. Atop her long green cotton skirt and white gauze top, she was trussed up with belts and beads and fringed pouches. She smelled of patchouli and vanilla. They headed to the kitchen where Free was putting a pan of cabbage rolls into the oven. He wiped his hands on his jeans and gave Pearly a shy hug.

"Hi. Glad you could make it," he said. Pearly smiled and pulled a bottle of wine out of her messenger bag.

"Libations," she said gaily as she placed it on the island in the middle of the room.

"Perfect. Let's imbibe," he said, reaching for the corkscrew in the drawer behind him. Emma fetched three wine glasses. They pulled up stools around the island. Free poured the glasses a third full and passed them around the table.

"So, how did you and Free meet?" Emma asked.

Pearly took a sip of wine and placed her glass carefully on the table. "At a Beltane gathering."

"Pearly was the most beautiful girl at the ball," Free said.

"Hush, chauvinist," Pearly countered sweetly. "I'm hoping I can drag him to another meeting tonight after dinner." She turned to Free. "You may not know that kNOxNUKES has been gearing up for more actions."

"I thought they folded," Free said.

"You and everybody else. Most people think our weapons are being dismantled. They don't know that the weapons industrial complex is hiding proliferation behind dismantlement programs. We're trying to keep a continued presence in Oak Ridge, but haven't been as vigilant since disarmament became the official party line."

"What sort of actions are you involved in?" Emma set out flatbread and homemade pesto.

"We watch. Most times that means we camp outside the reservation with binoculars and watch the trucks come and go. Then we follow them. We radio ahead when they get out of our area, and other NukeWatcher groups take over. That's the national group we're affiliated with. As a group we've successfully followed trucks all across the country. Lately though, the hotline is unmanned a lot of the time, so we can only report on our own region."

"What does that accomplish?" Emma took a sip of Pearly's malbec wine and almost smacked her lips. It was delicious.

"We are witnesses. We keep track of what goes where. Also, if one of those trucks has an accident and radioactive materials are spilled, we are the whistle blowers. Those fuckers get away with a lot because people aren't looking. You should come, Emma! There's a planning meeting tonight."

"Oh, thank you, but no. I'm already up to my ears in projects."

"I'll come," Free interjected.

"I was counting on it." Pearly looked at him suggestively.

The plates came out when the oven timer dinged. Like Free, Pearly had a finger in many progressive organizations. Between the two of them, they probably had a bead on every group in the region. Unlike Free, Pearly was heavily involved in the local alternative spirituality and healing communities. They chatted as they ate.

"I'll be reading tarot cards at the International Festival on June twenty-fourth. I'm helping out my friend, who is from Budapest. She's covering the history of her Romany ancestors. I'm the show and tell."

"Oh? How do you mean?" Free asked.

"Her ancestors read cards and told fortunes, so I'm setting up a table for readings."

"I was thinking about an urban farm demonstration, but I'm still waiting for my proposal to be accepted," Free said. "I guess they're debating whether it fits. Probably not, but I had to try. Maybe I should get one of my international friends to spearhead it."

Pearly nodded. "Right on. Whatever it takes to get the word out. Speaking of which, I'm hearing good things about your projects. I ran into a mutual friend at the co-op who was raving about your warehouse farm idea."

"Right now we're getting Emma's place in shape. We'd like to get the yard acting as its own little ecosystem. That's going to take time, but we have some great projects in the works right now toward that end."

"How do you plan to fund a warehouse?"

"Grants," said Free. "We're putting together proposals. Right now we're talking to downtown restaurants. Many of them have agreed to buy produce grown from the warehouse. In fact, they're giving me wish lists of vegetables to plan seasonal menus around. I'm putting together the blueprint and pricing the lights and grow materials. If this takes off, this warehouse can be our teaching arm and we can build other projects in less expensive places. There's a lot of win about the whole idea. Fingers crossed." Free crossed his fingers animatedly.

"Oh, let's consult the cards!" Pearly pulled a deck of tarot cards from the fringed leather bag hanging from her beaded belt.

She moved the plates aside, clearing a space for her cards. She held the deck sideways in her right hand as she deftly shuffled them with her left, causing a blur of silver rings and beaded bracelets. Emma was struck by the backs of the cards—midnight blue with stars, reminiscent of the design on Free's teepee, she thought.

In the center of the table, Pearly placed the first card. "Ah, the Eight of Cups. You are moving away from that which no longer serves you." The card showed a cloaked figure heading for the mountains and walking away from eight stacked cups.

She placed another card across the first. In it, a man was standing on a hill, beating back an attack from below. Recognition flashed on Pearly's face. "Well, it won't be easy. It will be an uphill battle, in fact. But with this card, victory is predicted."

Beneath those cards, Pearly placed another. "This is the root, the undercurrent of the reading. Two of Wands. A new enterprise, and look, you're holding the world in your hand as you gaze into the distance. An inspired idea coming into being. That sounds right."

Emma had to admit that so far Pearly's reading was interesting. She didn't know what she had expected, but not this. She sat forward, looking closely at Pearly, whose face had taken on an otherworldly, knowing look. She seemed to be in her element here. Emma was inclined to take her seriously.

Pearly placed another card above the rest. "Here at the top, we have the Queen of Pentacles. That's you, Emma. This card crowns you."

"Why do you say that?" Emma asked.

"Pentacles correspond to earth and the material plane. Queens are mature women. You've set out on this earth path, and you are directing this little project. You're a very grounded individual. This card reflects your possibilities in this matter. Earth Mama. That's your potential."

Pearly pulled another card and placed it to the left and center of the cards. "The Nine of Swords is your past. Emma, face your fears. That's the way through." On the card, an anguished woman in bed held her head in her hands while nine swords hovered above her.

"What do you mean?"

"You are very troubled. Something is causing you grief, keeping you up nights. Honestly, this card usually tells me that these fears are of your own making. Release them."

To the right and center of the spread, Pearly placed a card called the Magician. "This is the future. You have the creative power and energy to complete this task. You will do it! Magical forces will assist you."

More cards made their way to the table. "This is you in your undertaking, Emma. The Fool—the card of the Hero's Journey and limitless potential. Oh, it is a wonderful card for you now, Em. It says take the risk and step forward."

"Because I'm a fool?"

"No! Because you are an adventurer, a trend setter, not afraid to step off the cliff and risk your security and comfort."

"But I *am* afraid of those things."

Pearly looked a little impatient. "But you're doing it anyway! That's the very definition of a fool! The Fool calls for courage and creative expression, no matter what conventional wisdom says. He will be a vehicle to help you give birth to a new part of your life, without fear. That sums up what you're feeling right now. Right?"

She didn't wait for Emma to respond. "Okay, this is what opposes your task." She laid out three cards. The King of Swords, a king in a blue robe with a sword. The Five of Swords, a contemptuous young man looking at conquered foes in retreat. The Devil, a monstrous demon squatting between two chained prisoners.

"Well, here we have a stern businessman. He's going to cause a lot of trouble. He's paired with the card of betrayal and sneak attacks. And look. Not just him, but a Puppet Master."

"A Puppet Master?" Emma and Free moved in to look closer at the Devil. Chained at his feet were two miserable people. "That doesn't look good."

"Someone else may be calling the shots. Or maybe it will be an unpleasant, obsessed man who causes trouble. Either way, watch out for the King of Swords."

The next card caused Pearly to suck in her breath. "Ooh." Pearly squirmed ever so slightly. It might have gone unnoticed, but Emma was watching her closely. "Whoa. The Tower. Okay, some shakeup is going to happen."

Two people were falling out of a tower struck by lightning. They both looked at Free.

"What?" he looked up at them, startled.

"Nothing," said Pearly. Then, looking at Emma, she said, "Hey, at least it's not the Death card. Anyway, Death usually means transformation. The only time it means real death in *my* readings is when I draw the Four of Swords with it. And that's only happened a couple of times." She was babbling, trying to draw their attention away from the fiery tower.

"Ah, look at the next card."

Pearly seemed in a hurry to move on, so Emma let her. The next card looked as opposite as could be to the one before it. The Four of Wands depicted two people rejoicing under a canopy of flowers. "This is your outcome—peace and joy after challenge. The successful completion of your task."

With a satisfied flourish and looking at the clock above the stove, Pearly grabbed the empty pouch on her lap and moved to put her cards away.

"Wait, is that all?" After all that, Emma wasn't prepared for such an abrupt ending.

Pearly paused. "The cards are pointing to success after conflict. Well, I could draw a clarification card. I usually like to end the reading with a Major card anyway."

"What's a major?" Free asked.

"A Major card is one of the first twenty-two cards of the deck—like the Fool here—representing major life influences. It usually depicts the resolution of the matter in the outcome position. Since I haven't pulled one, it looks like the resolution is a little fuzzy. You're going to have some bumps in the road, but success is assured. Whatever the outcome of this work, an unscrupulous man will be involved. I call him that because the Five of Swords is a card of plotting and sabotage. Do you want to me to keep drawing?"

"No, you're good." Emma sat back as Pearly packed the deck into her pouch. What was she thinking, getting all wrapped up in something like this? It made no sense. She stood and started clearing the table. Free jumped up to help.

Pearly's many beads swished and her pouch fell to the floor as she got up. Free retrieved it from under the table and handed it to her. "We've got to get a move on if we're going to our meeting, Free." She grabbed plates and headed for the dishwasher. "One thing is for sure, Emma. Beware an unscrupulous gentleman in an authoritarian position."

With that, she headed for the door. "Sorry to eat and run, Emma. Free, I'll be in the car."

Emma reached to push Pearly's chair under the table when something caught her eye. Two cards had fallen to the floor. They must have fallen out of her pouch. She looked at them as she retrieved them. One was the Four of Swords. A figure lay in repose on a coffin, much like a body laid out for funeral viewing. The other card had the word "Death" written under a picture of a Grim Reaper on a horse.

"Here," Emma said, handing the cards to Free. "Give these to your girlfriend."

KNOXTOPIA
Plant a Garden. Change the World.

Nitty Gritty Basics

The best soil you can create and plenty of water are essential to the backyard garden. (Well, all gardens, for that matter.) One of the first things I did when I came to work with Emma was get the compost and rainwater collection going.

Dirt

Friends, if you want to save the world, you have to compost. Our world is in bad shape. It's like those starving people you see on the news. It is emaciated and near death. It needs food. Compost! As a responsible citizen of the Earth, you have a responsibility to recycle every bit of organic material back into the earth. It's an ecological imperative!

Emma already had a compost system set up when I got here—one big stationary pail in the back. Easy as can be. However those stationary pails take longer to compost. My first project when I started working for Emma was to build a drum composter. These rotating cans compost faster because you can aerate it quickly and easily. Just turn the tumbler a couple of times a week, and it will make compost in half the time.

I've seen some fancy plastic composters for sale in front of the Food Co-op. That's certainly an option. You can use just about anything to build your bin. I've made pallet bins and used plastic garbage cans. Drill holes in the garbage cans for aeration. (Steel cans work too but it's harder to drill the holes.) Some people just start a pile in the yard or dig a hole. I knew a guy who just dug it into a garden plot to be ready for the next season. He had a vegetable garden and he had a compost garden. He rotated them each season. Really, anything will do. It's not rocket science, people.

Well, here's the closest it gets to rocket science: the ratio of green to brown in your pile will make faster compost. I, however, have given you a handy cheat sheet below.

The best ratio of green (fresh, green or nitrogen-rich) to brown (dried or carbon-rich) is two to one, respectively. Honestly, I just leave a pile of brown material beside the compost and throw twice as much in when I dump food scraps or yard waste. This will help the materials decompose faster and not stink.

What to Compost

Add:

Manures (not dog or cat, and some say horse has lots of undigested seeds that can sprout)

Nitrogen-rich green materials such as fresh grass clippings, plant trimmings and remains, house plants and cut flowers, fruit and vegetable scraps, tea bags, egg shells, coffee grounds

Carbon-rich brown materials such as dry leaves, straw, wood chips, saw dust (add in very thin layers), cardboard (small strips)

Do Not Add:

Meat, bones, fish scraps, fatty foods including cheese, butter, oil, and salad dressing

Dog and cat feces

Diseased or insect-infested plants

Pernicious weeds such as crab grass

Weeds with pernicious seeds

Some people go to great lengths with their compost piles, checking the temperature and such. You can do that if you want to. My rule of thumb: If it stinks add brown materials. If it's dried out, add water. If it's too wet, add brown. If it isn't getting hot, add green materials or manure. (But don't worry too much about it because cold compost piles break down too. It just takes longer.)

Water

You may not have the means to buy all kinds of rainwater barrel art like Emma, but don't let that stop you from creating a water collection system for your citystead. I've made collection systems out of a 275-gallon plastic syrup container gotten at a soft drink bottling plant, as well as 55-gallon food grade barrels scavenged from restaurants (plastic or metal). If you can't find a generous restaurant or plant manager, hit up Craigslist. I've seen them made with new garbage cans too. And lastly, you can buy kits at home and garden stores now.

Short and sweet: Connect a plastic irrigation hose from your gutter to your barrel by cutting a hose-sized hole in the top. Add a smaller hole on the other side of the lid for overflow. (If using a pail and lid, it's a good idea to place landscape mesh on top of the barrel before securing the lid to keep bug, pests, and debris out.) Five inches from the bottom of your barrel, cut a spigot-sized hole and insert a water spigot. You'll want to insert rubber washers and metal washers on both sides before waterproofing the whole shebang on the inside. Fasten a hose clamp to the spigot threads inside the barrel.

See? Easy. You can pour water into a watering can or attach a hose. Your choice. If you want to set up more than one barrel, you can run a hose from the small overflow hole to the overflow holes of the second, third, and so forth barrels. (Put a spigot on each barrel for easy access.)

OK, so the above is bare bones. There are all kinds of instructions online for making your own rain barrel system. Start with *Mother Earth News*.

3 Comments

GreenByNature said ...

You can in fact use human manure for compost. Process it separately and use it on nonedible plants for two years. After two years, you can safely plant edible crops in it. At the very least, pee in your garden.

TeepeeFree said ...

That's a little advanced for the purposes of this blog, Green. I wouldn't recommend anyone try that without a lot of research.

GreenByNature said ...

I'm just putting it out there.

« CHAPTER 4 »

EMMA SMOOTHED HER SKIRT and adjusted her shoulder bag before she entered the realtor's office on Gay Street, just around the corner from Market Square. She and Free had finished the warehouse farm proposal over the weekend, and the next step was information gathering. Restaurant owners on the Square had been extremely enthusiastic about the idea. Most were willing to consider buying locally produced hydroponic vegetables if the price was right. Now she needed to get a look at available properties downtown, price them, and check out their zoning requirements. She had just toured the empty building beside the Indian restaurant. It was perfect for their needs. She followed the well-coiffed realty agent into Jackson Taurus Enterprises.

"Ms. Goode, if you'll have a seat, I'll tell Mr. Taurus you're ready to see him." The agent headed back toward the offices behind the reception desk, where an over-coiffed receptionist appraised her, probably wondering if Emma had enough money to be there.

Emma looked around the luxurious waiting room, which dripped of money and prestige. The owners had restored the historical building to its early twentieth-century grandeur. But for the stylish and expensive office furniture, she felt like she had stepped back in time. An elegant antique chandelier perfectly accented the high ceilings and elegant molding.

"Ms. Goode?" Jackson Taurus stepped past the reception desk and offered his hand. Here was more money, from his manicured fingernails to his tailored suit. His dark hair, brushed back fashionably from his angular face, was peppered with gray at his temples.

"I'm Jackson Taurus. Step right this way, if you please."

She followed the businessman and his realty agent down the hallway.

Taurus led her into a luxurious office. Emma took a plush seat in front of an expansive mahogany desk. The agent sat beside her. She couldn't help but notice that the desk, in fact, the entire office, was empty of personal paraphernalia. Taurus displayed no family pictures, no golf trophies, nothing.

"Now, Ms. Goode," Taurus began. "I understand you have taken a look at one of our Market Square properties." He opened a file and passed Emma a sheet with building specs, including lease information.

"I think it will serve our purposes well," said Emma, taking the paper.

"And those purposes are?"

"Hydroponics." Emma pulled open her briefcase and removed the business proposal that she and Free had written. "We'll need to do some minor modifications to the building. I need to discuss those with you."

Taurus flipped through the pages. His genial expression was replaced by a frown. "Ms. Goode, we were hoping to lease this building to a retail or restaurant enterprise."

"We are in the process of lining up nearby restaurants. Our plan is to sell the produce locally, producing whatever exotic vegetables they want for their menus. Today's trend is toward locally produced, fresh vegetables. The business owners we've talked to have expressed great interest. We're cutting the food miles to a few feet instead of hundreds or thousands of miles. That will be one of our selling points. It's an idea whose time has come."

Taurus closed the file. "Interesting. I see here you plan to apply for grants for your operating expenses. We're a business, not a nonprofit. I'm afraid you'll have to find something less … upscale." He stood, reaching for his briefcase. "Now, if you'll excuse me, Ms. Goode, I have another appointment."

***

Feeling unceremoniously dumped back on to the sidewalk, Emma turned to make her way back to the municipal parking garage.

"Ms. Goode!" Taurus' agent, clomping loudly in too-high heels, hurried to overtake her. "I'm sorry for that, Ms. Goode. Mr. Taurus has specific ideas for what he wants in his buildings. I should have warned you, but your idea seemed trendy enough to interest him. He's too blunt. I'm sorry."

"That's fine. Not your fault."

"He's especially upset lately. His wife died recently."

"Oh my. I'm so sorry."

"Well, his ex-wife. They were divorced, but still. Unfortunately, he owns most of the empty buildings on the Square. Here's an idea—maybe you could go through the mayor's New Visions project."

Emma felt the color drain from her face. That's the one place she was determined *not* to go.

***

"Why can't we go through Knoxville New Visions? I think that's a great idea." Free was listening to a rundown of Emma's day. She sat on the back patio while he measured and marked out frames for a beehive on a large piece of wood. The printed plans were laid out before him.

"Why are you doing that now?" asked Emma, looking more closely at what he was doing. "I thought the Farmers Co-op sold out of bees already."

"They did. I just couldn't wait to get started. Maybe we can find bees somewhere else. I haven't given up the search yet. We might find a wild hive." Free used a tape measure and charcoal pencil to plot out the pieces much like a dressmaker might lay out a pattern on fabric. "So, back to the mayor's project."

"You could buy a ready-to-assemble beehive instead of starting from scratch."

"Where's the fun in that?"

"We could grub out that overgrowth in the corner of the yard instead. That seems like the best use of our time right now."

"Why are you avoiding my question?"

Emma hesitated. "It really is the best place for the project. I understand that. It's just that I know some of the people at Knoxville New Visions, and I just don't want to go there. We have a history."

"Then I'll go to them. No problem."

***

Free and Emma sat in the waiting room of the New Visions office. It looked like any other office in the city's administration building, except for the posters. Reprints of posters from the WWII Victory Garden campaign adorned all four walls. *Sow the Seeds of*

Victory. Plant and Raise Your Own Vegetables featured a woman clad in red, white, and blue sowing seeds. Uncle Sam stood next to a garden with the caption *Uncle Sam Says Garden to Cut Food Costs.* And who knew there was a United States School Garden Army?

"So, you know these people?" Free asked.

"As it turns out, I don't. My late husband used to be the director. When I googled the organization last night, I found out that his old staff wasn't with the department anymore."

"The entire staff is gone?"

"Well, he just had a couple of people under him. But yes, they are gone. I didn't recognize any of the names listed on the website." To say she was relieved didn't even begin to cover her feelings when she realized she wouldn't be bumping into any old acquaintances—particularly Molly Steed. Had Molly been listed as a current member of staff, Emma wouldn't be sitting here right now.

A tall, blonde man hurried out of one of the inter-office rooms. He juggled his briefcase as he struggled into his jacket. "Hello, Free." Once the jacket was on and the tie smoothed, they shook hands. "You must be Emma," he said. "Hello, I'm Jerod Warner, assistant to the mayor. Nice to meet you. The mayor has agreed to meet with you today, so please follow me. This is an exciting development. He's a very busy man."

Joseph "Big Joe" Early was in the last year of his second term as mayor of Knoxville. In his early sixties, he looked like a big teddy bear, burly and loveable with white hair and bushy eyebrows. The old timers approved of his track record, for the most part. He provided plenty of handicapped parking and spoke out against new taxes in any form. The younger voters liked him for his green stance. He promised more green spaces and tax rebates for recycling. He was conservative but progressive—in short, a true politician who straddled the partisan lines of his constituents with skill and charm.

Emma had never met him personally, although she had heard plenty about him. Many an after-dinner chat centered on his manipulative maneuverings. Big Joe was both suave and cunning. David didn't approve of his tactics sometimes, but had to give him points for his ninja politics. As far as Emma remembered, David never mentioned dirty dealings on the mayor's part, just the cunning of a fox and expertise at playing both ends of the stick.

Introductions aside, Big Joe turned to Free. "Now, Mr. Byrd, tell me about your project."

With a look to Emma, Free launched into a description of the warehouse farm plan. Emma piped up to offer details of the project, from budgetary considerations to environmental impact.

"Six of the ten restaurants in the Square say they will join our vegetable co-op," Emma told him. "We are in talks with fifteen other restaurants in town.

As soon as the grants line up, most have promised to sign on. With some grant money for start-up capital, we will be able to keep this enterprise going."

"This hydroponics idea is quite expensive. Wouldn't traditional farming methods be more cost effective?" The mayor had a gentlemanly southern accent. His eyes showed courtesy and interest.

"With all due respect, Mr. Mayor, cutting edge ideas like this will be more expensive at first, but as they take hold, costs will likely come down," said Free. "Plus our costs will be passed on to our customers, who are in acute need of a year-round, quality source of green vegetables. They will pay premium prices to be able to say their vegetables are organic and locally grown, as in two doors down. It's a hot trend. What we don't sell, we can donate to food banks."

Jerod Warner pulled some papers out of his briefcase and passed them to the mayor. "Sir, here are some projections. We've looked at a similar setup in Chattanooga that seems to be doing well. The publicity for that project is overwhelmingly good."

"Chattanooga?" The mayor's eyes focused intently on Warner. "You're saying Chattanooga already has a setup like this?"

"Yes, sir." Warner shuffled through more papers. "Here's a write-up from their daily newspaper as well as copies of letters to the editor praising the project. They got an environmental commendation from Al Gore as well."

"All right, then," said the mayor. "I'm in. What will it take to make his happen?"

They talked construction and permits. Free had some sketches of hydroponic benches and a cursory description of the indoor farm setup. Warner brought out more numbers and projections. Emma supplied lists of vegetables needed by participating restaurants, including quantities and their exotic vegetable wish lists. Every time Chattanooga was mentioned, the mayor's ears pricked up and his interest soared.

"Where will this farm be located?" The mayor sat back in his chair and folded his hands over his ample middle.

Free and Emma exchanged glances. "That's not decided yet," said Emma. "We found a perfect location on the Square, but Taurus Enterprises isn't interested in leasing to us. We're still evaluating properties."

The mayor sat forward. "Leave it to me. You'll have your space. So, what else does ... ," he glanced at the proposal, "Knox Urban Evolution have in the works?"

"We're planning other projects now," Emma began, "but as yet we—"

"A solar power company in the Sunsphere," Free blurted out. "The Sunsphere is the most visible landmark in our city. We'd like to use that visibility to promote right livelihood in all its facets. We'd like to see socially responsible companies and nonprofit organizations up there to really put Knoxville on the environmental map."

Emma froze. *Please, please don't mention tilapia tanks now.*

"That's a novel idea, young man." The mayor smiled from ear to ear. "With your ideas we might even surpass Chattanooga as the Environmental City. Bring me a proposal as soon as you can. Warner, make this farm warehouse happen."

"Yes, sir."

And just like that, Knox Urban Evolution was in business.

***

Emma, Free, and Pearly celebrated with champagne and a cookout. Free grilled tilapia steaks and fresh, local vegetables. Pearly brought homemade bread and dipping sauce. Emma harvested greens from the garden. They congratulated themselves and wondered aloud at their luck.

"Free, how do you plan to work here, run a warehouse farm system, *and* start a solar power business?" Emma snipped sprigs from a potted rosemary plant for their fish.

"Good question. I think I'll have to beg an established solar business to join our merry band and recruit a legion of helpers." Free flipped the spatula in his hand playfully.

"No sweat," Pearly said lovingly as she kissed his cheek. "That's a walk in the park for you."

"Did something seem off about the Mayor's quick agreement to our plan?" Emma set places for each of them on the picnic table.

"What do we care? The important thing is that he agreed," said Free.

"I know, but he didn't give it much thought."

Pearly sliced the bread and arranged the olive oil and herb sauce on the platter. "I think he just wanted to get a leg up on Chattanooga. They are getting lots of attention and grant money for their Green City campaign. Maybe he wants to leave that kind of legacy. It *is* his last term."

"What's he doing after his term expires?" asked Emma.

"I heard he's going to make a run for the Senate. Ladies, hand me your plates. This fish is done."

They ate and drank until the moon rose high in the sky.

Free and Pearly cleared away the dishes and headed for the teepee. Emma stayed up for a while, watching silver clouds cross the face of the moon as she sipped her wine. Her head was full of plans for the project. She made a mental list of more upscale restaurants to approach. She wondered about the mayor's stake in this endeavor. For all his apparent interest, he seemed to be operating from an entirely different agenda. Was it merely political ambition? Was he just in a race to out-green Chattanooga, which had officially named itself the Environmental City? His excitement didn't seem to be for the environmental project, but for something else entirely.

***

Jackson Taurus called the next day while Emma was editing a local business owner's memoir. Since the ex-CEO of General Electric released his memoir a few years back, Knoxville's business elite decided they had stories to tell as well. Emma certainly didn't mind, as word of mouth about her editing skills landed her several lucrative jobs.

Taurus was unmistakably angry. "If you're still interesting in leasing the property on Market Square, come down to my office this afternoon to sign papers. Two o'clock."

"I thought you weren't a nonprofit business, Mr. Taurus."

"Fine, you don't want it then."

"Wait, of course we want it. My partner and I will be there."

At two o'clock sharp Emma and Free were sitting once again at the realty office owned by Taurus Enterprises, this time at a wide, shiny conference table. The amicable agent, a vision of professional style and efficiency, sat across from them smiling.

"Mr. Taurus sure made a one-eighty on this property," she said. "What happened?"

"I'm not sure," Emma said. "One minute the mayor was giving us city and state grants, and the next Mr. Taurus was offering the storefront. I'm wondering myself."

Before she could finish her thought, Taurus swooped into the room. With a sour look on his face, he dropped his briefcase and sat down. Without looking around, he produced some legal papers and pulled a pen from his front pocket.

"Sign these."

Free reached for the pen, but Emma stopped him. "Same terms agreed upon earlier with your agent?" Emma started reading the papers.

"Same terms," Taurus muttered. From his reddened face to his white knuckles, Taurus looked like a man who was doing something utterly, extremely against his will. "Now if you'll please sign."

Emma glanced at Taurus and kept reading. No way was he going to rush her into a bum deal. The room was silent as she flipped from page to page. Finally, she reached for the pen, signed her name, and scooted the papers over to Free, who also signed.

"You understand our carefulness in today's business climate," Emma said sweetly. Taurus glared at her, signed the papers himself, and handed them to the agent. "Take care of these, please."

The agent cautiously slipped out of the room. Taurus sat back. He looked steadily at Emma. "Mr. Warner was here yesterday. The city has guaranteed your lease up to a year. After that, the property comes back to me. I expect you to fail."

"How pleasant of you," Emma said. "Just what is your problem, Mr. Taurus?"

"My problem is that I'm a businessman in business to make money. I don't trade in schemes or impractical enterprises."

"Then why have you changed your mind?" Insulted, Emma was working hard to keep her cool.

"Let's just say the mayor convinced me."

"You would do well to follow the mayor's lead." Free's righteous indignation was making him brave. "We are developing a green plan for this city, with the mayor's full approval. Get behind it and you will be ahead of the curve. The mayor wants this."

"Really?" Taurus practically sneered. "And pray tell what does that plan include?"

"A warehouse farm system, for one," Free said, "and the reclamation of the Sunsphere. We plan to create a peace and social justice center there and lease offices to pro-environment businesses, with the mayor's approval. He's asked us to draw up the plans."

Taurus sputtered. "I haven't heard anything about this, and I oversee the Sunsphere property on behalf of the city." If Taurus was angry earlier, he was livid now.

"The mayor has asked only for a proposal," Emma said to Taurus. "Free, this conversation is premature. We should be leaving. Thank you, Mr. Taurus."

They left Taurus sulking at the mahogany table. As they passed the reception desk, the agent shook a key ring at them. "Here you go," she said cheerfully. "It's all yours."

Emma didn't dare look at Free until she had both a copy of the lease and the keys in hand. As they rounded the corner of Gay Street toward Market Square, she let out a whoop.

"Free! We did it!"

"Yes!" He lifted her off the ground and swung her around. Arm in arm, they headed for the warehouse.

KNOXTOPIA
Plant a Garden. Change the World.

Warehouse Project is a Go!

You heard it first, faithful blog readers. We have secured a downtown warehouse for the Knox Urban Evolution Gardens! Our hydroponic and rooftop gardens will supply vegetables for downtown restaurants, local stores, and the Farmer's Market. A percentage will be given to food banks.

Our building is on the northwest side of Market Square. We're leasing the rooftop and first floor with an option later for the second floor. On the roof will be a conventional rooftop garden. The first floor will house our hydroponic garden.

As you know, a hydroponic garden replaces dirt and weather with peat moss plugs and circulated water. In the absence of sun, we're using high-efficiency LED lighting. By eliminating transportation and natural fertilizers, we expect our hydroponic output to be $150,000 in retail food cost, producing 7 to 10 tons of food a year. (We're being modest here. We expect more.) This does not include the seasonal output of the roof.

Opponents of hydroponic gardening say that conventional electrical costs would soon put us out of business. We plan to prove them wrong. We will be using the new LED lighting, improving energy efficiency by 40- to 60-percent, as well as remote iPhone applications to continuously monitor our farm. We will keep you abreast of our process and costs as the growing season progresses.

We also plan to dedicate a bit of space to warehouse farming research. First we'll grow lettuce and herbs and raise fish in a water-based aquaponic system in a greenhouse set up on the roof. We'll gauge its effectiveness as a potential large scale production.

The KUE Gardens Co-op is well underway. We have six local restaurant members and a couple of whole foods stores lined up. Excess crops will be sold at the Farmer's Market. We are planning our growing season now with requests from our members. And lastly, KUE Gardens is a learning center. We will be conducting city farming workshops on a regular basis.

Contact us if you would like to be involved in this very local food experiment. Forget the 100-mile diet. How about the 100-yard diet? This is going to be as local as it can get.

7 Comments

GreenByNature said ...

Congrats!

PearlyMussel said ...

Can't wait to get started! Way to go, sir!

TeepeeFree said ...

It's not just me. All hail, Emma, my amazing partner in crime. And Pearly, my lady and helper.

PearlyMussel said ...

;-)

AnnieL said ...

I appear to be blocked from comments under the name Annie_Speaks, my blog for and about Knoxville night life. Is this a mistake?

BradB said ...

Way to go, man!

GoodeAbe said ...

Congratulations to Emma and Free on this major coup. I look forward to much blogging about this project.

« CHAPTER 5 »

VERGIE DELL WAS ALWAYS counting the days until her husband Jay came home. It seemed like he was gone more than he was home. If she didn't know better, she would think he was making up excuses to stay away. But he wouldn't do that. He was a God-fearing man and a good husband. Besides going to church with her when he was in town, he had plenty of interests that took him away from home. He belonged to the National Rifle Association, and he had a huge gun collection. He collected knives, too. Since he was a hunter, he had an uncommon fascination with things like night vision goggles and camouflage Ghillie suits. He was always going to this gun show or that monster truck rally. He was a busy man when he wasn't on the road.

Jay made just enough money so that Vergie didn't have to work outside the home, and for that she was grateful. But as each empty day stretched before her, she was always looking for something to do. God forbid she should have idle hands. She cleaned her house. She read the Bible. She watched church on the television. She cleaned her house some more. Some nights she went to Bible study. Tent revival season was in full swing. Bible School season was right around the corner. She could hardly wait.

Sometimes, just to feel closer to Jay, she would look at his collections. She didn't do it because she liked those things, but because they were Jay's things. It was sort of like smelling his shirts when he wasn't there. She missed him. She looked at his gun catalogs, opened and closed his collectible pocket knives, and looked out the window with his binoculars. She especially liked to look through his night vision goggles in the evenings. It helped her keep tabs on the neighborhood without anyone noticing. Heaven knows that evil can creep in from any direction. That's how she saw the harlot with the landscaper. She got a good look at them and their sinful shenanigans, too.

She tried to talk to Emma Lee Goode about the evil in her backyard, but she wouldn't listen. Ever since David died, Emma Lee seemed to be going downhill. Well, if Jay died, Vergie would be sad, too. Not sad enough to quit caring what the neighbors thought, though. That was just crazy.

Vergie tried to alert the authorities, but they didn't listen either. They just implied that she was being nosy. The nerve! God called it vigilance. She put Emma on the prayer list at church. The demons were at Emma's door, after all. She confronted the landscaper. She didn't know what else to do. She was scared, and not just for Emma. She didn't want those devils right next door.

That's why she went to the message board at NoOtherGodBeforeMe.com. She needed guidance from her fellow Christians. Shepherd3 told her to give them Christian tracts and pray for them. Exodus22_18 told her to burn the house down, because how could a good Christian let evil like that stand? Vergie didn't like either of these solutions. Apparently, neither did the other board members because the entire thread erupted into scripture slinging and threats. Proud_fundie blamed it on the Democratic president. Everyone could get behind that, but unfortunately the damage was already done. A few people were banned from the list forever. The thread was locked. Just when Vergie thought she wasn't going to get any good advice, she received an email message on her Hotmail account.

To: jesuslover1968

From: g0ds_warri0r

Subject: Heathen extermination

I see from yor NoOtherGodBeforeMe.com profile that u live in knoxville. Me too. The Fellowship of Christian Warriors can help u. We meet at teh old holiday inn off Mercury Dr every tues at 8.

†God Saves†

The next Tuesday, Vergie wasn't very happy about missing Rev. Floyd's special seminar, "Fixing the Gays: God's Plan." He had promised to reveal the top ten most AIDS-infested cities in America. Homos need to repent, and they need a lot of prayer. She had hoped to get some ideas about what to say to the effeminate boy who bags her groceries at Food City. Curiosity about this fellowship trumped the seminar however. Plus, her friend, Truda, promised to take notes and call her with a report on the seminar tomorrow.

It was a good thing she had a long memory, because the Holiday Inn hadn't been the Holiday Inn for a long time. Now it was the North Mercury Motel. The neon sign blinked off and on as she pulled into the parking lot, flashing No Merc y Motel in bright red script.

Armed with her Bible and purse, Vergie stepped into the hotel lobby. A balding, middle-aged man sat behind a long folding table in front of a meeting room. Propped beside the table on a folding chair was a black board with white plastic letters. It read, "Fellowship of Christian Warriors."

Vergie approached the table. The man cleared his throat. "Can I help you, ma'am?"

"I'm here for the meeting."

"Please sign in." He slid a clipboard across the table. A handwritten sign-up sheet contained 20 or so names. She added hers, along with her address, phone number, and email address. Under

"Member?" she wrote "No," and noticed that everyone else wrote "Yes." Under "Who invited you?" she wrote "g0ds_warri0r."

"The meeting has already started. Please have a seat." He handed her a pamphlet and waved her into the meeting room with a weak smile. She glanced at the front of the tract. Bold letters proclaimed, "The devil is a loser. Are you a faithful soldier of Christ at war with him? If not, YOU are a loser too." She slid it into her Bible, and headed for the front of the room. Empty folding chairs took up the entire space. Sprinkled in the front rows were the other signed-in guests. At the dais was a man dressed in camouflage with a red beret. On a tripod next to him was a homemade poster with a picture of a saber and a rifle forming a cross encircled by the words, "Fellowship of Christian Warriors." Beneath the logo, she read "Reverend Buford Gunn."

"We must awaken the warrior and put on the armor of God!"

The crowd, though small, was responsive. A smattering of amens rose from the group.

"Some mock the idea of Christians at war. We reject such limp-wristed timidity as ungodly rubbish!"

"Yes!" cried the audience.

"We are on order from the Captain of our salvation. We are in the trenches facing the vast forces of evil Satan and perverted men. In First Timothy 1:18, we are told, *This charge I commit unto thee, son Timothy, according to the prophecies which went before on thee, that thou by them mightest war a good warfare."*

"Amen!" "Hallelujah!"

"We may not retreat. We will never get discharge papers. All that is left for us is to take up our mighty weapon, the King James Bible, and defend the Lord against the evil among us!"

Hearty cries of "Amen" and "Yes, brother!" erupted from the crowd. The good reverend was already on a roll, and Vergie settled into her chair to listen.

***

Morticia and Pearly were unlikely companions in the bookstore café. Morticia, a pale girl wearing lots of black mascara, wore a long black skirt, a revealing blood-red bustier, and black spiked boots that laced up to her knees. Her black hair, obviously dyed, hung down her back. Black fingernails completed her look.

"They will be mad if they know we're talking to each other about this," Morticia said as she anxiously fiddled with her nose ring.

"It can't be helped. This has gone too far." Pearly sipped her soy chai latte. "When Crow and Spyder fight, the whole pagan community goes berserk. They've been around long enough to know better."

"You'd think." With a shrug, Morticia took a slurp of her quadruple espresso.

"So what do you propose we do to make peace? Spyder is pretty agitated that Crow threw a wrench into his Beltane mojo."

"There was no wrench-throwing. She simply thought Spyder should have cast a circle or something, and talked about it ... endlessly, with anyone who would listen. You know how they bicker."

"Talked about it? More like stirred the rabble. Now he's an energy vampire? But who started those friggin' baby sacrifice rumors against Crow on the message board? Good gods, even the pagans believe that stuff now? I'm still trying to figure out who sent that message." Pearly stabbed at her whipped soy cream with her green straw. They sighed simultaneously.

"You should let me ask around. I can read auras and can pretty much tell when someone is lying. Anyway, people get stupid when they log onto those message boards," said Morticia. "The Internet is a curse."

"Agreed. And it's gone on too long. I can't believe how it's escalated."

"Before you know it, the magical people will make so much noise that the mundanes will notice. Then we'll all start losing our jobs and having our children put in foster care. So what can we do before it gets to that? How do we unify the community again?"

"Again?" Pearly snorted. "This will be the first time."

Morticia grinned wryly. "Smart ass. Most pagans are perfectly lovely people. Hell, for that matter, most Christians are, too."

"And Jews and Muslims, etcetera. We just live in a town with a high ratio of nut jobs. Speaking of nut jobs, there's that dude again."

Morticia turned in the direction Pearly's straw pointed to see a scrawny man duck quickly behind his open newspaper. "What a loser," she said to Pearly. "We see you, asshole," she said loudly. She turned back to Pearly. "So, what do we do about Crow and Spyder?"

"Well, how about a street festival or something? We'll invite all the traditions in town to set up booths. You know, give them all equal time. We can let Spyder and Crow feel like they're spearheading it. Have music, vendors, food. Invite the community at large so they can see we're not the bogeyman."

"Hmm, a unity event. That might work. Puts Spyder and Crow out there together. Doesn't spotlight one more than the other. It'll work wonders for the community. Yeah, that could work. How soon?" Morticia pulled up the calendar on her phone.

"Fall, if we can manage it. Hey, the International Festival is coming up on June twenty-fourth. We're actually setting up a booth for tarot card readings. We're sharing a booth with Julianna from Budapest. It's not as large scale, but it's soon. At least we can get them working together. I'll bring up the idea of the Unity Fair while we're there."

"Then it's done. You talk to Spyder and I'll talk to Night Crow."

***

Days passed and projects on every front appeared to be progressing well. Plants were growing. The homestead was flourishing. The restaurant co-op was coming together. That was when the news broke in the local newspaper.

"Green Racketeers" Line Pockets with Warehouse Farm Project, Say Opponents

KNOXVILLE, Tenn.--A new warehouse farm project proposed for the Market Square district is being hailed locally as a bold, visionary move for the city. Several opponents of the unique plan to grow organic hydroponic vegetables in a downtown building made their concerns public at a Rotary Club meeting last night.

"At the city's expense, this enterprise will be growing expensive gourmet foods for the city's ritziest restaurants," said Rep. Darrell Andaryl, a Republican. "And I might add these restaurant owners are long time contributors to the mayor's campaign. Just because something is called 'green' doesn't necessarily mean it is the best thing for our city. If the city is going to subsidize farming, let it be about farmers and underprivileged people who need food, not about gourmet chefs and the rich."

Andaryl, who has long been opposed to Mayor Joseph "Big Joe" Early's green platform, called for a protest against the farm, citing the need for more information, and a debate on both sides of the issue.

Knox Urban Evolution Gardens is slated to go online in early June. As part of the Green City Plan, the city has awarded the project a $400,000 grant as seed money. This money will go toward an expensive plant watering system, including a rain water recycling system, and solar panels to provide energy in the building. Heirloom and endangered vegetables and herbs will be grown and sold to area businesses and residents. Plans also include a rooftop garden.

"The green movement will make somebody very rich, and that is what it's all about," said Andaryl. "I for one am not buying into it. I heard a scientist just the other day saying that his lab had proven that the green movement is just a hoax, but their report was not allowed to be seen."

Andaryl's comments were generally well received at the meeting. "I'm not against recycling, particularly, but I can see now that individuals are stepping in to make a buck at the expense of the ill-informed," said Ansel Rucker, Rotary Club treasurer. "I don't speak for the entire organization; however, this is my opinion."

A representative from the mayor's office had this to say: "While Representative Andaryl is entitled to his opinion, the Mayor's forward-thinking green plan has many facets that will benefit many sectors of our society. KUE Gardens is just one piece of the total pie. Locally grown, heritage foods are certainly in demand at many restaurants, but this project also will supply food for the Farmer's Market and local pantries."

Recent allegations that the project's manager, Free Byrd, was arrested seven years ago for growing and selling marijuana in California has alarmed Andaryl and other city leaders.

"So the city is subsidizing a pot farmer now?" asked Andaryl.

No record of Byrd's alleged California arrest exists. Opponents to the farm warehouse, who have nicknamed the project the Grow House, say Byrd was a minor at the time of arrest, therefore the record has been expunged. Byrd could not be reached for comment by press time.

"Once again political alarmists are sounding the battle cry," said Councilwoman Faye Bleu, a Democrat. "Rather than coming to the table with legitimate concerns, they are throwing their hissy fits in front of the local media. It's time for adult conversations rather than public temper tantrums."

City representatives meet next Tuesday. Bleu said the KUE warehouse was not as yet on the agenda.

***

Emma called Free over to the computer as soon as he came in for coffee that morning.

"Shit," he said.

"Free, I know we have some asshole representatives, but what's this about a California arrest?"

"Yeah," Free looked away. "Well, I was seventeen at the time."

"It's true?" Emma took the news like a slap to the face.

"My folks were hippies. They weren't morally opposed to marijuana. We decided it would be a good cash crop. There was a market in California at the time for medicinal herbs of all sorts. We lived off the grid. My folks agreed with me that supplying medicinal marijuana to the pot clinics would provide the best return for my time and effort. It was a great idea."

"It was an *illegal* idea."

"Yes, but I have to reiterate that I had my parents' permission. It was part of my homeschooling, a business building class. I learned a lot. My dad used to joke that all businessmen were criminals, so I was in good company."

"Free, this is out in the public. It could ruin us. How did the records get expunged?"

"I worked community service until the day before I turned eighteen. I was doing lots of work in the soup kitchen anyway, so they counted that as time served. Pretty much I just kept on with life as usual. I made weekly trips to volunteer in the soup kitchens and did trash pickup. The judge liked me, I think."

Emma held her head in her hands, her elbows on the desk. "Why weren't your parents implicated?"

"Oh, they wanted to be. They wanted to take their responsibility for what had happened to me, but I reasoned with them until they saw my side. I was a minor and could get it off my record. They, on the other hand, could go to jail. It took a lot of convincing, but they finally gave in. It was touch and go for a while."

Emma looked at Free in amazement. "You crazy, crazy boy. But I love you all the more for that story. Now, you get that we can't tell the public anything about this? It will kill our project. How did they find out if the charges were erased, anyway?"

"I don't know."

"Who could have told them?"

"That was a long time ago. Someone had to go digging for that information."

"Free, I'm going to ask you like you asked your parents. Please, for the sake of our community work, don't tell the press anything about this. They'll just drag you through the mud and our credibility will be trashed. The warehouse project is at stake. They won't find the records, so I think we can contain it. Can I get your word?"

"Sure, Emma."

He meant it. She could tell he really meant it.

***

It only took a couple of hours before local talk radio was all over the news. Emma wouldn't have known except for Pearly's call later that morning.

"Oh man, they are giving KUE hell on the radio," she said. "Tune in to 1310 AM."

Indeed they were. The two morning show personalities were knee-deep in a discussion about the validity of the Green Movement in general, and about the city's "secret pot-growing racket" specifically. Emma listened as she washed the morning's harvest of spinach.

"Leave it to the liberals, Brent. We should have known it would only be a matter of time before there were pot plants in the City-County Building. What's next, goofballs from candy-dispensing machines in the halls of the courts?"

"I agree, Al. This is what happens when liberals have control of the government. The very fabric of our American culture begins to unravel. Let's take a call. Roger from Halls. Hello. You're on the air."

"Brent? Al?"

"Yes, hello. We're here. What is your question or comment?"

"Abortion! I want to talk about those girls sitting in the projects on welfare having baby after baby so they can draw more government money."

"Roger, our topic today is 'The Green Movement: Hoax or Help?,'" said Al.

"I think it's a crime how they sit home and watch TV and draw those government checks. All those babies have different daddies."

"So you think they should get abortions?" asked Brent.

"No! Abortion is a sin!" said Roger.

"Roger, our topic today is the Green Movement. Do you have anything to say about that?" Al sounded as though he was directing his stern tone more to Brent than Roger.

"How much do they get extra every month when they have another kid?"

"Thank you, Roger. Next caller." Brent clicked to the next caller. "Altruda from Powell. What's on your mind, Altruda?"

"To answer that last gentleman's question, they get about $50 extra in their cash benefits each month. Not hardly enough to—"

"Thank you, Altruda."

Click.

"If you have comments about the Green Movement, call us at 555-TALK. Is it a hoax? Let us know. Vergie from Knoxville. You're on the air."

"*Before I formed you in the womb I knew you.* Jeremiah 1:4. That there is definitive proof that God is against abortion."

Al sighed. "Thank you, Vergie. Do you have anything to say about the Green Movement, the KUE Grow House, or the mayor? Or that kid who is project manager. The one who grows pot? What's his name, Brent?"

"Free Byrd, Al."

Al sniggered.

"Oh sure," Vergie said. "He's got a marijuana garden growing in my neighbor's backyard against the fence. I'm looking at it now."

Emma's colander clattered into the sink. She didn't even turn off the water as she raced out the backdoor and dashed toward the back fence. She ran the length of the yard peering through stands of shrubs and plants, looking into flower pots, and checking all the way around Free's teepee. That's where she found them—three towering potted bushes with five-fingered leaves. They stood tall in the middle of the pallet where Free stored plants for his landscaping business.

"Omigod, omigod," she whispered frantically as she moved closer. Vergie was probably reporting to the radio show right now that she was out here. She moved closer to the plants and pinched off a leaf.

Wait, something was wrong.

She sniffed. No, this isn't marijuana, she thought. She pushed back the leafy stems and examined them carefully. That's when she noticed the plastic labels from the nursery buried halfway in the potting soil. "False or Spider Aralia, *Schefflera elegantissima*."

Emma sat down hard on her butt as the adrenaline rushed out of her system. She laughed out loud. For a split second relief flooded her. Then she realized the damage Vergie had just done. Right now talk radio was having a field day about marijuana growing in her backyard, or maybe abortion. Either way, it was not good. Emma broke off a five-fingered branch, snatched a plant label out of the pot, and headed for Vergie's front door.

Vergie's eyes widened as she opened the door, the cordless phone still to her ear. "I'll call you back," she said hastily, and clicked the handset off. "Hello, Emma Lee, honey. What can I do for you?"

"You can get your talk radio cronies back on the phone. I know you have them on speed dial. Tell them that's not pot in my backyard. It's false aralia." She thrust the evidence at Vergie, who took it cautiously. Vergie read the label. She looked at the plant. She pinched a leaf and sniffed it.

"Um, where'd you get this, honey?"

"In my backyard. Right where you told those radio people Free was growing marijuana."

"Why, Emma Lee, that wasn't me."

"Vergie, just shut up and call them back. Tell them."

"I'm sure I don't—"

"You meddling fool! Call them!"

Vergie's mouth dropped open and her face lost its color. She hit two buttons on the keypad of her phone and waited, all the while staring at Emma. "Vergie from Knoxville. I'm calling with a comment about the pot grower." She fidgeted as she waited on the line. Emma glared at her. In less than a minute, she was connected.

"Yes, it's Vergie again. Al, I'm afraid I gave you some misinformation about the pot grower. That isn't marijuana in their backyard." She glanced nervously at Emma. "Well, my neighbor has brought evidence to my door. It looks like it's a plant called false aralia, but it is an easy mistake. It looks just like the other."

She paused, listening to the voice on the other end of the line. "Yes, she's standing here at my door." Pause. "No, I didn't go to the garden with her." Pause. "Well, I suppose she could have switched plants. Really? They have decoy plants?" She looked up at Emma.

"Aargghh!" Emma snatched the phone from Vergie's hands. "Listen, you are slandering me over the air waves, and I would like it to stop. There are no pot plants in my yard."

She could hear the deejay talking excitedly at her as she handed the phone back to Vergie and headed back home. When she entered the kitchen, he was still chattering away on her radio.

"Of course she denies it," he said. "The lady doth protest too much, methinks.' Would you agree, Brent?"

"I agree, Al."

And Vergie's voice: "There's always something going on over there. Just last week—"

Emma switched off the radio.

***

Free picked up Pearly after putting in a sweaty morning installing fruit trees at a local Montessori school. The owner wanted edible landscaping, and Free had talked her into planting heirloom pears and pawpaws, both on the Slow Food Arc of Taste, a list of foods facing extinction. She wasn't sure about the pawpaws until Free mentioned that the kids would have firsthand knowledge of the fruit while singing the Pawpaw Patch song. Her eyes sparkled as she thought of the show-and-tell possibilities. Free and Pearly were headed now to the warehouse, singing the song as they drove along.

"Pickin' up pawpaws, put 'em in your pockets, way down yonder in the pawpaw patch." They sang and giggled all the way downtown.

Free cruised the side streets for free parking, but there wasn't any to be had today. He usually worked after hours when the parking was free. Today, he was accepting a delivery of lights and other electrical supplies, so paid parking it was.

As they turned the corner to the Square, they could see a commotion down at the other end.

"Is there an event here today?" Pearly asked.

"Don't know of one." As they walked toward the warehouse, they noticed that some of the people held signs. "Hey, it's a demonstration. Maybe we know them. Let's see if we can join the cause." Free took Pearly by the hand and pulled her along.

A man with a sign watched their approach from a knot of fifteen or twenty people. He pointed at them and yelled, "There they are!" Free looked at his sign. It was a pot leaf inside a red circle with a slash. As he and Pearly got even with the crowd in front of the warehouse, a woman's voice cried shrilly, "You want tomatoes? Here's your tomatoes!" A volley of tomatoes came hurtling at them. Free took one square in the face. Pearly was immediately pock-marked with red splotches. She screamed, and they hustled inside the building.

"What was that?" Free's voice was a mixture of panic and astonishment as he locked the door behind him.

"Why are they picketing us? Us? *We're* the picketers!"

"It's that radio show, Free. I told you." Pearly answered from the bathroom, where she wiped at tomato stains with a wet paper towel.

"But how did they mobilize so quickly? Even the most aggressive leftist groups around here can't get it together this fast."

Pearly walked toward the storefront, still dabbing at her blouse. She handed Free a paper towel. An old man with a can of spray paint was painting something on the window. They watched in fascination as the words "Pinko Commies" materialized, reversed from their side, in Krylon's mambo pink.

"You'd think they'd come up with something else after all these years," she said. When they walked up to the plate glass for a better look, another barrage of rotten fruits and vegetables smacked against the window. They jumped back. A particularly pulpy tomato slid down the window, smudging the old man's art. That started a ruckus as the old man yelled at the crowd. Arms were flailing, and voices were rising.

"We better call the police, Free. They're getting nasty."

"Have you ever heard of the Right organizing nonviolence training? No. That's why these things get so out of control." Free was still wiping at his face as he dialed the police. "Hey, is that old man wearing a gun?"

The press caught wind of the commotion when the call went out on the police scanner. Before too long, three police cars had pulled into the Square along with one newspaper reporter, his photographer, and three TV news crews. Pearly noted the absence of the talk radio station, the perpetrators of all this in the first place. "Forget source material and little things like facts when you can operate solely on hearsay and speculation," she fumed.

After talking to Free and Pearly inside, the police stepped outside to disperse the crowd. When the first tomato hit a beefy police officer, backup was called and the demonstrators—the ones who hadn't hot-footed it out of there—were cuffed and led to a police van.

The news crews were in high gear, working the story from every angle. They interviewed demonstrators. They interviewed shopkeepers. They interviewed a couple of the homeless who lived in Krutch Park. They stopped some skateboarders, who made hand signs and mugged at the camera. They even talked to the old man as he was being led away by the police. "Attica!" he screamed. A couple of reporters even knocked politely on the warehouse door, but Free and Pearly didn't answer. Free worked distractedly on wooden benches for the hydroponic setup, stopping often to watch out the front windows.

Their delivery came at four o'clock. Most of the demonstrators were gone, but a few arrests were still being made. A crowd had gathered to watch, so a policeman stood guard at the door while the FedEx man made his delivery. For once, Free was grateful for a police presence.

At six o'clock. Free turned on the radio and adjusted the dial until he found a simulcast of the local news. KUE Gardens and today's demonstration was the lead story. Free and Pearly listened glumly.

KNOXTOPIA
Plant a Garden. Change the World.

Sunsphere Project in the Works!

Lots of dreams are coming true here at Knox Urban Evolution. Our farm warehouse is well underway. We're busy with redesign, installing fixtures, procuring seeds, and the like. Our planting plan is nearly complete. Things are great.

But wait! We have another project to announce. We're bringing the Sun back to the Sunsphere. We plan to open a solar power business/think tank there as well as offices for other green city projects and nonprofit groups. KUE soon will be overseeing and developing the Sunsphere property at the World's Fair Site.

Our city has never known quite what to do with our most notable landmark. Created for the Knoxville 1982 World's Fair, the spherical, gold-paneled building sits on top of a 266-foot steel truss structure. The theme of that World's Fair was Energy Turns the World, so we want to bring solar energy back to the Sunsphere. Forget Bart Simpson's Wigsphere! (You've watched that totally fictional episode of *The Simpsons* where Bart visits Knoxville and discovers a wig shop in the Sunsphere, right?) The Sunsphere will offer a one-stop shop for all your solar power needs, from panels to photovoltaic cells. We'll give your home a solar makeover and send the crews out to implement it. Whether you want to outfit your entire home or power a transistor radio, we'll have it all.

Lots of plans are swirling around this project. We won't take over until the current lease is up, so stay tuned!

In Other News: Container Tomatoes!

Speaking of large bulbous orbs, we've planted some tomatoes in containers. In honor of our Sunsphere project, I planted a Yellow Brandywine in a container by the door. It's pretty awesome to just open the backdoor and grab a handful of warm tomatoes to throw in your salad *as you're making it.*

Many experts will tell you to use only determinate tomato plants in containers. These are bush plants that grow three or four feet high. They only produce fruit for a couple of weeks, though, then fade out when the flowers set. I generally put indeterminate plants in containers. They will produce all season and die at the first frost. However, I have to stake them, and they will need at least a 5-gallon container. They also need to be fed a lot. I add manure tea or compost tea to water. Careful not to overdo it. If you see signs of burn, cut back. We planted indeterminate plants.

For organic container tomatoes, Emma had several bags of high end organic potting soil in her basement, so we used that. This is definitely the gourmet variety of potting soils. Of course, you don't have to use fancy-schmancy potting soil. Not many of us have these $23 bags lying around. You can use compost! (I know you have some. If not, get some!) You can simply combine your best soil with cured compost, leaf mold, rotted sawdust (from untreated wood) or a long list of other organic ingredients. Google it. Here's how to do it:

1. Choose organic heirloom plants.

2. Fill your pot with the soil of your choice. Make sure you have a drainage hole in the bottom.

3. Scoop a deep hole into the center of your pot.

4. Take the seedling out of its container and place it into the hole deep enough so that it is buried half way up the stalk. This is important for getting a stable, healthy plant. Add additional dirt if needed.

5. Water thoroughly. Container plants need lots of water. We usually water ours daily.

(Manure tea about once a week. Watch for overuse. Plants will exhibit a "burned" look.)

6. Add tomato cages when you plant for when the plants get larger and need additional support. When the plants get large, I place bricks around them or back them up against a hay bale or wall—anything to give them additional stability. They sometimes get top heavy.

7. Don't throw away your plant tags. You'll wonder which varieties you're eating later.

8. Try not to drool too much during the 75 or so days it takes for your little pieces of sunshine to ripen.

Manure/Compost Tea: Use cured compost or manure from a horse, cow, chicken, or goat. Rabbit is very high in nitrogen and will burn quicker than other manures. If you use it, dilute it more. Fill a bucket two-thirds full of water. Add manure until the water level reaches the top. Let it steep for a day or two, stirring once or twice. When you're done, let the solids settle to the bottom, then dip out your tea. Dilute it with water until it is about the color of weak tea—pale brownish-yellow. Compost the leftover manure.

A word of warning: Meat-eating animals like dogs and cats can transfer pathogens to your food through their manure. Avoid these.

8 comments

GoodeAbe says ...

The hits just keep on coming! Congratulations to the team and thanks for container gardening info. I have a small terrace and have been experimenting myself. Wonder if I could get away with manure tea in a downtown apartment? LOL

TeepeeFree said ...

Well, as long as your neighbors don't complain! Keep it small and use a plastic can with a lid. Try it out and report back.

GreenByNature said ...

I wouldn't use trucked in potting soil if I were you. Keep it local, man. Even Zoo Doo would be better.

TeepeeFree said ...

I agree wholeheartedly on the local idea, Green. We were using up what Emma already had lying around.

Radio_Al said ...

This Sunsphere idea of yours is stupid, as is the Mayor's Green Initiative. Everyone tune to 1310 AM Talk Radio for the scoop behind these crooks. *Al and Brent in the Morning*, 10 a.m.

PearlyMussel said ...

???

SpeakAnnie said ...

Watch yourself, Radio_Al. He'll block you like he blocked Annie_Speaks, a blog about Knoxville night life.

KnoxvilleBoi said ...

What? What'd you do to the Wigsphere?

« CHAPTER 6 »

DINNER THAT NIGHT WAS a solemn affair. Not even the recent baby kale harvest cheered them up. Emma told Free and Pearly about her experience with Vergie and talk radio, and they told her about the downtown demonstration. Since the local news ran repeatedly on cable until the new newscast, they were able to watch the segment about the protest. News footage showed protesters waving their signs, resisters being carted off, reaction from passersby, and the vandalism. Pearly and Free could barely be seen peering out from inside behind the graffiti.

They exchanged troubled glances. Just as Emma turned off the television, the phone rang. It was Jackson Taurus.

"Ms. Goode, we need to discuss something. Can you meet me for lunch tomorrow?"

"I believe so, Mr. Taurus. What is this about?"

"I'll fill you in tomorrow. I'll meet you at noon at Downtown Sushi."

"Fine, I'll be there." Emma went to bed that night fully expecting to lose the lease on the warehouse. She decided against telling Free until after she met with Taurus.

***

Emma arrived at Downtown Sushi before Taurus, so she got a table by the door. She nervously checked the buttons on her cream silk blouse and smoothed her navy jacket over her matching slacks. Taurus strode through the door precisely at noon. He looked around the dining room, spotted her, and headed her way.

"Ms. Goode." It was more a statement than a greeting. He unbuttoned his expensive jacket and sat down across from her.

"Mr. Taurus." Emma placed her napkin in her lap. The waitress scurried to the table as soon as Taurus picked up his menu. Obviously he was a regular and expected no less. Taurus ordered for Emma as if that were totally his right. Emma was determined to choose her battles, so she didn't protest. She waited for Taurus to speak.

The sake came immediately. Likewise, the seaweed salads and edamame. Had he called ahead? Did they always cater to him like this?

Taurus still hadn't spoken. Emma could take it no longer. "Why have you brought me here, Mr. Taurus?" She reached for her water.

He looked at her coldly. "We need to talk about your husband."

Startled, Emma set down her glass and stared at Taurus.

"There was a lot you didn't know about your husband."

"I think I know plenty."

"You know plenty because I made sure you knew. I sent you the video tape after your husband died." Taurus continued to eat as though he were discussing the weather.

Emma thought she was going to be sick. She had never mentioned the tape to anyone. She had never even watched it all the way through before destroying it. "What? Why?"

Emma could see the cold rage in his eyes. "Molly was my wife, dear. Didn't you know that?"

"Was? No." Confused and hurt, Emma replayed images in her mind. The agent told her his ex-wife had died recently. Molly Steed was his wife? That would account for his hostility from the moment they met.

"She died in a car accident recently, but I've always known about her and your husband. She smuggled two things out of his office the day he died. One was the sex tape. The other was evidence that he and Molly were taking bribes from contractors to overlook codes transgressions and greenwash their projects. I found both items later in Molly's office. I confronted her. She threatened to expose some of my own ... ah, indiscretions if I were to make any of it public knowledge. I kept silent for my own sake."

"Then why did you send me the tape?"

"Revenge, I suppose. I wanted you to hurt as much as I did when I found out. I still loved her then. The grief and betrayal were immense, as you found out. Everyone thought David Goode was such a saint, but he was tainted just like the rest of us. The mayor had him in his back pocket. In fact, I'm certain the bribes went straight to the mayor."

"Don't bring the mayor into this. You're furious with him for pulling your Sunsphere contract. Sounds like sour grapes to me."

"Oh, yes. I'm angry at the mayor, but that doesn't change the facts. Your precious mayor is one of the most corrupt politicians in the country. This 'good ole boy' routine of his is just an act. He couldn't care less about your green garbage."

"I refuse to listen to any more of this." Emma got up to leave. Taurus grabbed her hand under the table and pulled her back down. "Listen, Emma," he whispered hotly. "I'm not done. Back off the Sunsphere project, or I *will* go to the press about the history of Knoxville New Visions."

"What makes you think I care about Knoxville New Visions any more, and what's more, why do you think the press would even be interested?"

"Just how interested are they in your hippie friend right now? I think your little organization is very newsworthy at the moment."

Sudden realization dawned on Emma's face. "You leaked the information about Free." She wrenched her hand out of his grip. "How did you get access to expunged records anyway?"

"I called in some favors."

"Sorry, I still don't care."

"Well, maybe you will care if I send your sons their own personal copies of the video tape."

Stunned, Emma stared at him in disbelief. "How could you do something like that?"

"I've got a lot of money riding on my plans for development of the Sunsphere and World's Fair Park. We were signing the contract for a deal worth millions of dollars when you and your stupid friend swooped through with your ridiculous plan. The mayor was behind us until then. How do you think you got your warehouse? He promised to back my plan if I gave it to you. Now you Three Stooges are planning to take over the Sunsphere as well."

Emma stood.

"Back off the Sunsphere," he hissed.

She nodded and made her way for the door.

***

Emma called Free from the restaurant parking lot and arranged to meet him at his job site. He was installing a green sunfish pond at a residence in Fountain City, very near her home. Free rambled on during the conversation about talking the owner into native rather than exotic fish like koi. He was very proud of himself. When Emma hung up, she cried.

So much of this PR nightmare was focused on him. The fact that he now could discuss the merits of native versus exotic fish was amazing—and very much the kind of person Free was. He had a passion for a better world. He created his utopian vision for Knoxville one person at a time. He imagined a good world, and he had complete confidence that others would embrace this world if he could only share what he knew. Free was a modern day seer, a lone voice in a world estranged from its roots.

The fact that he could step away from the current smear campaign about himself made what she had to do that much harder. His eyes were on the vision, the utopia that he knew humans were capable of creating. His own reputation didn't even register as a blip on his radar as long as he was doing what was right.

Wiping her eyes, Emma pulled into the small driveway on Greenway Drive. Free said the owners were at work, so she walked around to the back where he was working. Already he had dug the hole for the pond. It looked like a splat, not a circle. Free said the more surface edges there were, the more wildlife would flourish on the banks. Now he was inserting the black lining. He looked up as she rounded the house.

"Emma, hello! How are you this beautiful day?" Free dropped the lining and climbed out of the hole. He motioned for her to sit on one of the wrought iron benches that faced the pond. "Isn't this nice back here? These benches were already here, so they decided they would like a nice pond so they could sit and watch the fish."

Emma couldn't waste time on small talk. She was about to burst with anxiety. "Free, I've got to talk to you." Her hands shook as she pulled her handbag off her shoulder and set it beside her on the bench.

"Emma, what is it?" Free, noticing the red, puffy eyes, took her hands in his. Concern showed in his face.

"We've got to pull out of the Sunsphere project."

"Why?" Free sat back, surprised.

"Because—," Emma couldn't hold back the tears. She sobbed. Free shifted closer to her and awkwardly put his arm around her shoulders.

"Tell me, Em. Tell me what's wrong."

"I can't take all this subterfuge and trickery. I can't bear to see you dragged down like this. Taurus has threatened me. He's accusing my husband and the mayor of criminal activity. Free, I'm sorry, but it's not worth it. I can't go forward with our plans. I'm not like you."

"Em, don't cry. You're more like me than anyone else I know, better even." He patted her shoulder comfortingly. "Tell me what he said. As for the mayor, I know a lot of good guys and I know a lot of bad guys, but he seems to fall more in the good guy category. But let's not worry about him." He produced a red bandana out of his back pocket and handed it to Emma. She dabbed her eyes and took a deep breath.

"Free, my late husband David apparently did some bad things. I didn't realize how bad until I talked to Taurus. I had lunch with him today. I thought he was going to yank our lease, but it was worse than that, far worse."

Free rubbed Emma's shoulder, silently encouraging her to continue.

"You see, David had an affair with Taurus' wife." Fresh tears erupted as Emma spoke the words for the first time.

"That's not good, Emma, but it's really not blackmail material. Taurus has as much to lose as you in revealing their affair. And no offense, but that was a long time ago. Maybe the public wouldn't care after all this time."

"That's not all." Emma sighed deeply and looked at Free. "There was a sex tape of my husband and his wife. He has copies. He's threatened to send them to my sons if I don't back out of the Sunsphere project."

Free stood abruptly, his fists clenched. "Why would that nasty asshole do that? What kind of disgusting subhuman is he?"

"I know. I know. He has a lot of money riding on development of the World's Fair Park, and the mayor promised his cooperation. Now it looks like the mayor has yanked the rug out from under him. They were signing contracts when the mayor offered us the Sunsphere."

"Well, that sucks and everything, but doesn't that sort of thing happen in business all the time? Deals fall through every day."

"Apparently not without a dirty, mud-slinging fight when it comes to Jackson Taurus. The good news is that he isn't threatening our warehouse project, just the Sunsphere. And Free, he is the person who found the information about your arrest and leaked it to the press. He wanted you and me to be newsworthy before he dropped his bomb on me. He has some proof about my husband's business dealings that he is willing to share with the press as well."

"What kind of business dealings?"

"David accepted bribes from contractors who were greenwashing their projects. He supposedly falsified environmental impact reports so that they would be eligible for grants, I guess, but mostly so communities wouldn't oppose the projects. Taurus will make that public while we are front and center in the press. Exposing you was just his way of showing me he is very capable of destroying our credibility."

"Can that bastard sink any lower?"

"Oh yes, I think he can. I'm sure he's dug up as much dirt as he can on both of us, and he's not afraid to use it to his advantage. The fact that David was doing the same kind of work that I'm doing will just cast a shadow over everything we do."

Free sat back down. "I don't care what they say about me. I'm going to do the right thing."

"Oh, Free. I know this about you. I love this about you. You're like a son to me." The words were tumbling out of Emma's mouth. "But I can't let Taurus send that tape to my boys. I can't let them feel the same shock that I felt. I have lived with so much shame and guilt over the years. I can't let that happen to them. They idolized David. I can't! I have to stop this. I have to back out of the project."

Free was silent for a while, deep in thought. He turned to Emma. "First, I have to tell you that your sons are grown men, and even though you feel a need to protect them, they have their own karma to work out.

"Second, this is why we do the work. We want to reinvent our culture. We want to live in a humane, trusting world where people treat each other with care and dignity. It's not just about cleaning up the environment. It's more than a healthy planet. We need healthy souls, Emma. We need to live our lives with love and respect.

"Men with black hearts will do anything to get their way. They will use the misfortune of others for their own advantage. Sad, gut-wrenching things happen to people, and that is bad enough. Then these conniving men step in to make money off the grief and misery of others. Don't you see the evil in that? Are we going to perpetrate that cycle? Can we meet this threat with a heartfelt response and stand with dignity? I think that is our responsibility here. I don't want to see men like Taurus threaten anybody's children ever again. We need to break the cycle. We are strong enough to do this. And Emma, I'll stand with you."

Emma sobbed harder into Free's shoulder. He held her tight. "You tell the boys first. Then Taurus has lost his power over you."

***

"What now?"

Emma pulled into her driveway behind a police car. A tall, trim officer emerged just as she stepped out of her car. Clean shaven and tan, his brown hair was sprinkled with silver.

"Mrs. Goode?" He asked as she drew nearer.

"Yes, can I help you?"

"I'm Detective Andrew Green." He flashed his badge, "We've had a complaint about some suspicious plants in your backyard. Mind if I take a look?" When he took off his sunglasses to address her, his deep brown eyes were all business.

Emma glanced at Vergie's house. "Well, I guess I know where that complaint came from."

"I'm not at liberty to say, Mrs. Goode. Can we step around back?" He made a gesture for her to go before him, so she dutifully stomped to the backyard, not paying attention to whether or not he was following. When she got to Free's plants, she turned to face him.

"Take samples if you want. These are ornamental plants called false aralia." Emma crossed her arms and waited.

Detective Green squatted down by the plants and inspected them casually. He stood. "Yeah, this isn't marijuana."

"Thank you!" Emma couldn't hide her vindication.

The detective stood up and pulled a notebook out of his coat pocket. He began to write. "Problem with your neighbor?"

"Don't get me started, Detective. Have you *talked* to her?"

"Yes, I have." He smiled a crooked grin then. "She also complained about this teepee here. I told her that was out of my area, but I'm sure she has notified the correct department by now. FYI."

"Sorry she wasted your time. She seems to have made me her personal project lately."

Detective Green pulled a card out of his pocket and handed it to Emma. "If she continues to harass you, let me know. Maybe I can talk to her."

"Thanks, Detective."

"No problem." There was that grin again. This time it reached those brown eyes. He turned and made his way back to his squad car.

***

As luck would have it, Leonard Sheldon was getting an exclusive interview from Free Byrd for the UT *Spotlight*. Leonard pulled into Free's driveway early the next morning. Byrd had called him late last night inquiring if he wanted the story. Leonard got a boner at the thought. If he could get this interview before his ten o'clock Communications Law class, he could transcribe the interview, and write the story tonight at the *Spotlight* office before deadline.

After checking his handheld tape player for batteries and stuffing two fresh AA batteries in his front pocket, Leonard scooped up his pens, reporter's notebook, and camera from the passenger seat and headed for Free's teepee. Last night, Free had told Leonard to come on back when he got there.

Free sat cross-legged in the center of the dwelling deep in meditation when Leonard knocked, or rather flapped, at the canvas door. Slowly he stood. "Mr. Sheldon. Welcome."

Leonard self-consciously extended his hand as he entered the teepee. "Call me Leonard, Mister Byrd. Thanks for seeing me again."

"Well, our interview experience was so pleasant at the restaurant co-op meeting and the story so even-handed that I knew you were the reporter I needed to talk to."

Free offered Leonard a cushion beside the one he had just vacated. They both sat down. Leonard crossed his legs awkwardly.

"I have some conditions before we start, Leonard. It is very important to me to get my side of the story out to the public. If you have any intention of sensationalizing what I say, be honest now. Some very unscrupulous people are threatening the work we are trying to do here. It is not about us. It is about the work. I will tell you the truth behind all the slander, but the major thrust of this article *has* to be the vision we are striving toward. Also, don't interview Emma Goode until the article runs. I doubt she would give you an interview anyway."

Leonard cleared his throat. "Mister, um, Free. As a reporter, I must tell you that I have a responsibility to report the news with objectivity. It would not be ethical to let the subject of a news story decide the slant of the story. It would also be unethical and one-sided if I didn't pursue other angles of the story."

Free smiled. "You have just said the magic words, 'responsibility' and 'ethical.' Turn on your tape player. I have a story to tell you."

When Leonard emerged an hour and a half later, he started to snap pictures of Free and the teepee. He walked around the yard with Free, taking more pictures as Free described the rainwater, compost, and raised bed systems. Leonard chased a chicken around the yard for the best photograph, and set up a shot of Free holding a baby goat while standing by the beehive. Leonard was particularly happy when the elusive chicken ran through the shot just as he pressed the camera button.

He and Free shook hands as Leonard headed for his car. He had enough material for an editorial about Free's dilemma as well as an on-going series about the greening of Knoxville. He might even call it that, "The Greening of Knoxville," after the '70s classic book *The Greening of America*. Not only would he make A's in editorial writing, magazine article writing, and photojournalism, but now he had a research topic for his law class (which he had missed). He would explore activist journalism, specifically how reporters, as the information gate-keepers, must take responsibility when setting the agenda in public discourse.

KNOXTOPIA
Plant a Garden. Change the World.

You've no doubt heard a lot about us in the local news lately. Journalist Leonard Sheldon states our case eloquently in a recent UT *Spotlight* article. My name is Free Byrd, and I approve this message.

Green Smear: City Planners Take Green Opposition to New Low

KNOXVILLE, Tenn.--In a bid to discredit Knoxville Mayor Joe Early's Green Initiative, some city politicians and businessmen have launched a campaign to vilify key project organizers. At the heart of the issue is Knoxville Urban Evolution (KUE) Gardens, a hydroponic farm setup in the heart of downtown. Opponents to the project say cronyism is at the center of Mayor Early's plan to fund the gardens. They also say known criminals head up the undertaking.

"At the city's expense, this enterprise will be growing expensive gourmet foods for the city's ritziest restaurants," said Rep. Darrell Andaryl, Early's longtime political rival. "As I've said before, these restaurant owners are long time contributors to the mayor's campaigns."

Andaryl argued in a recent *Press* article that rich restaurateurs are not the best recipients of city handouts.

"If the city is going to subsidize farming, let it be about farmers and underprivileged people who need food, not about gourmet chefs and the privileged," he was quoted as saying.

Andaryl, who has long been opposed to Big Joe's Green platform, called for a protest against the farm, citing the need for more information and a debate on both sides of the issue. He says the criminal past of project organizer Free Byrd is the "final nail in the coffin of this ill-fated initiative."

While public debate on issues relating to local politics are the bread and butter of civic governance, the *Spotlight* takes issue with the tactics Andaryl and other city leaders have taken to spread their message. Their strategy can be summed up in two words—smear campaign.

While these antics might have gone unnoticed, Andaryl made the mistake of enlisting Al Scheeder, radio personality of *Al and Brent in the Morning*. Scheeder tells anyone who asks that the Tennessee representative requested he "discuss" personal details of Byrd's life on his show.

"Representative Andaryl asked us to showcase the types of people the Mayor has chosen to head his initiative," Scheeder said. "We were happy to point out the injustice. Lawbreakers have no place in local politics."

When asked how details of Byrd's past were obtained for the radio show, Scheeder said a representative from Andaryl's office told him to pick up a packet of information from a downtown real estate office. He did not specify which office.

Byrd does not deny the allegations. However, critical parts of this story were left out, he says. Byrd was a licensed grower who sold medical marijuana to a legal dispensary in Arcata, California. However, he obtained that license by falsifying his date of birth. The then 17-year-old listed his age as 21. That was his crime. He sold marijuana under the auspices of the California government but otherwise followed every rule to the letter, according to court transcripts given to us by Byrd. His punishment for that crime? Public service for a year. The judge put the brunt of the blame on the State of California for not screening its caregivers more vigorously.

So yes, a crime was committed by a minor who served his sentence. Government agency wrists were slapped, and the records were expunged, only to be dug up by a Tennessee representative years later to serve his own political ambitions.

We do agree with the Representative on one point when he said: "The Green Movement will make somebody very rich, and that is what it's all about."

Yes, Rep. Andaryl, it will make many somebodies very rich: The citizens of Knoxville. The growers. The buyers. The eaters. The community. Sustainable farming practices will make us all richer in myriad ways—ways more important than money.

Gary Lawrence, the director of the Seattle Planning Department says it better than we ever could: "Sustainability is a political choice, not a technical one. It's not a question of whether we can be sustainable, but whether we choose to be."

Knoxville, it is our hope that we will choose to be.

1,333 Comments

TOP COMMENTS

God*Is*ALL said ...

I don't know how you pot-smoking, granola-chewing nitwits got in the City Council Building, but I want you out. You are a disgrace to the town.

(99 Comments <u>View</u>)

PearlyMussel said ...

The prevailing paradigm is dying a slow death. These naysayers are fighting tooth and nail as they go down with their archaic, unsustainable ship. Wake up, conservatives. The world is changing. It has to change or we all die. Is your immediate comfort more important than clean air, clean water, and healthy children?

(303 Comments <u>View</u>)

Radio_Al said ...

Don't believe this propaganda! The lunatics are running the asylum. Tune in for *Al and Brent in the Morning* 1310 AM.

(63 Comments <u>View</u>)

<u>VIEW ALL COMMENTS</u>

« CHAPTER 7 »

EVEN THOUGH EMMA DESPISED talk radio, she had taken to listening in each day to see what the latest scandal about them might be. The morning show had been raving about KUE exclusively for the past week. Vergie was becoming a local celebrity in the talk radio world with her close proximity to Emma's backyard and her willingness to speculate and stretch the truth. "Lie" might be a better word, her willingness to lie.

This day's broadcast started like many more before it. After a few chords of a dramatic theme song, Al came on the air. "Welcome to Talk 1310. I am Al Scheeder. Joining me is Brent Tandy. Today's topic is the mayor's involvement in the KUE Grow House. Did the mayor inhale? Brent, who is our first caller?"

"Al, our first caller is Rebecca from Knoxville. Rebecca, you're on the air."

"Yes, thank you. I just want to say that you are totally irresponsible news people. Your reporting is biased and untrue."

"We don't pretend to report facts, Rebecca. We are giving people an opportunity to voice their opinions," said Al.

"My opinion is that you are bigoted assholes and—"

Click.

"Thank you, Rebecca. Brent, who is our next caller?"

"Oscar from Halls. Good morning, Oscar," said Brent, too cheerfully.

"Al and Brent, I just want to say that your show is a blight on the face of society. Why are you picking on two people who just want to make the world a better place?"

"To whom are you referring, Oscar?" asked Al.

"Emma Goode and Free Byrd. Leave KUE Gardens alone. They are doing good—"

Click.

"Next caller. Remember, our topic today is 'Did the mayor inhale?'" said Al.

"Our next caller is John from Farragut. Hello, John." Brent was sounding a bit suspicious now.

"John, is your call regarding the mayor's drug use or the KUE Grow House?" Al sounded a little frantic.

"Yes, Al. It is. Mayor Early is one of the most effective mayors this town has ever seen. You are blatantly telling lies about him to further your own political right-wing agenda. It's a disgrace."

"He thinks Mayor Early is one of the best mayors this town has ever seen, Brent."

"I heard that, Al."

"John, we are just presenting the facts as they are revealed to us."

"Facts? You just said your show was all about opinion."

Click.

"Next caller," said Al. "Phil from Knoxville."

"Al, if I ever see you outside that radio station I am going to kick your ass. Then you will get an idea how hurtful your words can be."

Click.

"We will return to today's topic, 'Does the Mayor Smoke Marijuana?' after these words from our sponsors."

In his eagerness to switch to commercials, Brent left the sound booth microphone turned on. Al's voice could be heard over the Bateman Cleaners spot. "Brent, ask each caller what they want to discuss before you throw them to me. The fuckers are hijacking our show." Then, "Shit! Turn off that mic."

Fumbling was heard before a definite click stopped transmission from within the sound booth.

The commercials ran much longer than usual, and for the first time in a while, Emma laughed.

***

Pearly and Free peered around the corner into Market Square as they exited the parking garage. They liked to see what they were walking into. One could only sustain so many rotten vegetable stains on one's clothing, said Pearly. The daily risk of flying tomatoes was making them gun-shy.

On this day, the protesters were still there, but something odd was happening. One crowd stood defiantly in front of the warehouse door throwing nasty glares and the occasional insult to another crowd, huddled on the other side of the mall. Free recognized the signs on the far side of the Square. The red-slashed pot leaf sign was beginning to look tattered, but it was still recognizable. Free tried to get a look at the signs carried by the new group. One said, "Food Not Bombs." With a sigh of relief, Free and Pearly hurried toward the warehouse door.

As they got nearer, a cheer went up from the new crowd. Free and Pearly were patted on the back and congratulated as Free unlocked the door. "What is all this about?" he asked the young woman closest to the door. "We're taking our city back," she replied with a smile.

From inside the warehouse, Pearly read the new signs to Free as he transferred basil plants into the hydroponic setup. "'Hate is not a Family Value.' That's an old reliable. 'Bullies Go Home.' 'Green Power to the People.' Oh, that's a good one."

Pearly beamed with pleasure at the counter protesters, obviously delighted by the show of support. Every time the original protesters started to creep across the Square, the counter protesters mock-lunged and shouted at them until they backed off.

Passersby began to gather around the two groups. Many obviously sided with the protesters of the protesters. Some began to jeer at the old group. When the insults were beginning to get violent, a team from the new protesters gathered around the agitated insult-slingers. They talked them back to reason. "No problem, man. People have a right to assemble and make their opinions known. Just like us." The discussion usually ended with "We cool, man?"

They talked to the over-heated person as long as needed, until the situation was diffused. This time Free beamed with pride. "See? That's what nonviolence training will get you. I'm so proud right now."

***

It started almost immediately after Leonard's editorial. Not only was the talk radio show swamped with angry callers and the counter protesters amassing downtown, but green projects were cropping up everywhere.

Almost overnight, bike racks and old, refurbished one-speed bikes were unloaded around town. A bike pump was affixed to each rack, as were signs saying "Honor System. Borrow these bikes. Drop them off at the rack closest to your destination. Save the planet and get healthy." Included was a map of drop off/pick up points and an appeal for the donation of unwanted bikes in any condition. Each bike was engraved with a serial number on the handlebars and the words "Property of Bike Borrow," presumably to prevent resale or pawn.

Beautiful flower gardens began cropping up overnight in obscure places like street medians and unused city planters. Placards were placed in each one, saying "Guerilla Gardens. Making Green Spaces from Waste Places. Please enjoy and follow suit!" Used, clean tin cans and other containers with labels reading "Take One" held packets of seeds.

A legion of knitters sat in the square knitting gigantic, green wool cozies for bike racks, trees, and fire hydrants.

Two wildlife aquaculture professors showed up at a city-county meeting with plans for public tilapia tanks. They were like sidewalk aquariums, only the fish were edible. Benches would be installed nearby so pedestrians could watch the fish. Their presentation was complete with diagrams, costs, yields, and harvest, with the fish being donated to food banks and homeless shelters. They planned to exchange grades for student involvement, eliminating the need for city expense. They had grant proposals in hand and ready to submit once they got the city's approval.

Following their presentation was a botany professor with a proposal for free public orchards. He also planned to offer establishment and upkeep of the orchards as part of his class curriculum. His presentation mapped ideal places for such spots, including Krutch Park downtown. The Arbor Foundation had agreed to donate fruit trees.

The *Metro Gnome* and *Press* had a rash of paid advertisements and classified ads for shares for existing and new community gardens, city farm demonstrations, and other green undertakings. Community bulletin boards were likewise burdened with green ads of all kinds.

The evening news that week reported two more proposed warehouse farms and, as a public service, listed the city's recycling programs and drop-off points. A surge in recycling left the city's sanitation workers struggling to keep up with demand.

Someone paid for a billboard that read "Knoxville Urban Evolution Gardens, The Right Thing at the Right Time." (A day or so later, a nearby billboard read "Billboards are the Scourge of the Earth." Owners of the billboard company gladly put up the sign. The local EarthFirst! group had offered them a hefty fee. They were subsidized, of course, by the national organization.) Finally, sandwich boards were placed at each end of Market Square. They read "Yes to KUE Gardens" and "Get Out of the Red, Go Green."

Free got a call from the producers of *More at Four*, the local news magazine show, for an interview about KUE projects. They wanted to do a satellite feed from the warehouse. Local news celebrity Marita Dunne showed up with perfectly coiffed hair in a blue business suit, her cameraman in tow. She clomped around the vegetables in their hanging frames in high heels, smiling profusely into the camera while asking Free about hydroponics, insect control, and harvests.

Emma got several calls for interviews, one from the *New York Times*, who often reported on the urban farm trend. They were particularly interested in the polarization of the town brought about by the warehouse project. Early signs were that it was going to be another one of those crazy-southern-people articles, this time with a city homestead twist.

Free was in high demand as a consultant for the warehouse project and other green projects. He was in hog heaven. Pearly's tarot card reading business got a bump as well. Seeing her in the news reminded her clients that they were due for another reading.

As the days passed, the trio stayed busy. Each morning Emma, Free, and Pearly were delighted with the news, rather than depressed and worried.

The gloom that pervaded the days immediately after the first news article was replaced with a new drive to push forward. The vile sentiments of their bitter opponents seemed like nightmares washed away by the light of morning. Yes, things were looking up.

Mornings on Market Square were still tense. Both sides of protesters were thinning in number, but the diehards still showed up each morning. Whoever showed up first got the spot by the warehouse door. Lately, the original protesters showed up first. Free thought it was because the Right had a whole lot more staying power than the Left, who often got distracted by other things and slept in a lot.

The protests became more of a general political stump for the two groups, rather than a specific protest against or for the warehouse. New signs read "Frack Off, Gasholes" and "Planned Parenthood, Planned Murder." Free found that he could go about his business undisturbed most of the time. The police presence on the Square was heightened, and the groups rarely interacted. Usually violence only erupted over the issue of who got to set up by the warehouse door. When either group missed the opportunity, they reacted in predictable ways.

When the Right lost out, they usually tried to start something with the Left, who sat in purposeful silence. If that made the Right angry, they poked the opposition with their signs. If that was ignored, they hit them with their signs. That's when the police jumped into the fray.

When the Left got there too late to sit by the door, they would sometimes walk to the door and just sit down. The Right would try to drag them away, but dead weight is hard to move. At times like these, the Right would sometimes succumb to delivering blows. The police would then jump into the fray.

On the days that the Right wore pistols in holsters, the Left generally congregated on the other side of the mall. On those days, the police spent a lot of time checking for weapons permits and hauling off the occasional illegal gun carrier.

Market Square business owners were complaining. Forget this circus, they said. The real issue is the bottom line, and these clowns are driving away business. It was true. After the initial novelty of competing protesters wore off, most people just avoided them. The downtown bar-hoppers were still amused, but they, as a whole, tended to enjoy watching and making fun of such flagrant acts of stupidity wherever they might find it.

Fortunately, the Chamber of Commerce had a Market Square office. They began to put pressure on the City Council. The police assigned to downtown were instructed to get rougher on the protesters. They began enforcing ordinances that made their lives quite uncomfortable. They measured their distance from the doorways and fire hydrants. If protesters were inside the prescribed off-limits areas, they were arrested. They enforced the vagrancy laws. If anyone spent the night on the Square, they were arrested. Curfew was enforced.

Children caught on the mall with their parents during school hours were collected by the truant officer. The police found hundreds of ways to put the squeeze on the protesters. Every day the number of protesters dwindled. Only the most extreme political activists returned day after day.

KNOXTOPIA
Plant a Garden. Change the World.

Hi, I'm Emma, here for a rare blog post. Free is swamped with the warehouse project and grassroots organizing. When he's not at the farm warehouse, he is at one meeting or another helping get many more green projects off the ground.

We are overjoyed that the fruit of our current trouble is the incredible green explosion we're seeing in this town. From the impromptu bike share to the UT Tilapia Tanks, we are humbled at the outpouring of love and energy toward our Mother Earth. Free says this is how the Revolution starts—at the grassroots. He asked me to share a quote from Margaret Mead.

Never underestimate the power of a few committed people to change the world. Indeed, it is the only thing that ever has.

Pearly is compiling a website to include a searchable database of all the green projects starting up all over town. We'll be sure to share that with you when she's done. In case you haven't been keeping track, a lot is going on. I can't even keep count of all the community gardens popping up. I see a bartering website, KnoxBarters.com, has been developed. Besides public orchards, the University is planning a food forest near downtown. Every day I hear of more community meetings to discuss green projects. The Urban Farm Animal League is up and running, and ready to help you navigate city ordinances concerning your chickens, bees, goats, and rabbits. And this is the short list. So much is going on everywhere. Please share your own green projects in the comments. We would love to hear about them.

I hope you will get out to the World's Fair Site on June 24 when the mayor unveils his Green Initiative. Free and I were invited to sit in on some of the planning meetings. You're going to be blown away! Chattanooga will have nothing on us. They've made us promise not to reveal their plans until the press conference, so I urge you to go. You will be proud of your town. A big thank you also goes out to Deputy Mayor Wanda Hopper. She is the greenest voice in this town, hands down. If there is a woman behind the man in Knoxville's green journey, it is Ms. Hopper. Her vision and common sense has been the driving force behind the mayor's green legacy.

So, Knoxville, keep up the good fight! We'll see you at the press conference.

2,003 Comments

TOP COMMENTS

AmericanDave said ...

I never thought I would say it, but I am ashamed to be a Knoxvillian now. The leftist commies have taken over our town. I say we take it back.

(357 comments View)

Paradigm_Shift said ...

Hooray for KUE! Hooray for Mayor Early! Finally Knoxville is moving into the 21st Century.

(358 Comments View)

KnoxvilleBoi said ...

Really, I'm serious. Is the Wigsphere gone?

(115 Comments View)

VIEW ALL COMMENTS

« CHAPTER 8 »

THE MORNING REP. ANDARYL was told his ratings were slipping, he realized that the Knoxville Green Movement was gaining momentum at an exponential speed. He called in his assistant for some strategic brainstorming.

"I've dropped five points. Primary elections are in August. How the hell did this happen?"

"Well, sir." His assistant cleared his throat and pushed his glasses up on his nose. "*Mornings with Al and Brent* spun out of control. It was more than the public could take. It was the backlash. Their speculation sickened the casual listeners. The hardcore listeners decided to retreat so as not to appear mindlessly vulgar and obsessively politically polarized."

"I thought talk radio appealed to the mindlessly vulgar and obsessively politically polarized."

"Well, apparently it offends the genteel Southern sensibility of at least half the town."

Andaryl snorted derisively. "Fuck Al and Brent. How do I get my ratings in the polls back up?"

"You could resurrect your green racketeer rhetoric. That's what got Al and Brent going in the first place. Well, that and your personal request that they jump on your bandwagon to discredit the mayor's initiative by any means necessary."

"That damned Jackson Taurus was supposed to give the idiot the information so as to keep me out of the picture. How did my name even get into it? I was doing Taurus a personal favor by giving him those details. End of story."

"You had me contact the radio show from this office, sir. I sent Al to Taurus to get the information. Al apparently doesn't know what the word 'confidential' means. Maybe Mr. Taurus didn't adequately impress on him the need for discretion."

"Taurus wants rid of Big Joe as much as I do. I heard Taurus is thinking about running for mayor. He wouldn't make a mess of things at this stage. And I don't need Early running for the same Senate seat as me in the future. He's too damned popular. Neither of us needs the bastard breathing down our necks in upcoming elections."

"Perhaps it was our choice of messenger."

"No shit. Al's a goddamned moron. Taurus is quite the conniver, though. I have to admit that was a master stroke, asking us to dig up dirt on that hippie and Goode woman. It really got the rabble going. He's going to make a great politician. He couldn't have done it without me, though. Do you realize the favors I had to call in to get those records?"

Andaryl steepled his fingers as he sat in thought.

"I need to keep Taurus on my radar. Get me anything you can on him."

"Yes, sir."

"Where's my next speech?"

"This Sunday at Golf Range Baptist."

"Perfect. I need a speech about man having dominion over nature. After that I need a soft green platform with biblical leanings. Save the Earth, but Man is still supreme. And I want that Al Scheeder destroyed for the PR nightmare he's caused me."

"Destroyed, sir?' The assistant paled.

"Yes. Unemployed. Disgraced. I don't want him to ever find work in my district again."

"Yes, sir." Turning on a heel, the assistant was visibly relieved.

***

Mornings with Al and Brent had been in reruns for the last several weeks. The sponsors were pulling out, saying the show had gone too far with its gossip-mongering. Word on the street was that the mayor, with his long memory, had a list of every sponsor prominent on his desk. Radio execs pulled the plug on live shows until public sentiment settled down. Brent continued his tech work behind the scenes. Al was on temporary leave. He spent a lot of time at the library.

Al was very upset. How dare they try to suppress the voice of the people? Organized news was nothing but a bunch of liberal hippies who insisted on spreading their hippy-ness into living rooms everywhere. His rights were being trampled. Whatever happened to free speech? Oh right, it was only free if the network owners agreed with you.

On this day while perusing the communications section, he pulled a copy of *Pirate Radio* off the shelf. What he read as he sat on the rolling stool between the shelves made a lot of sense. He had access to a room full of old radio transmitter equipment at the station. He was off the air, not locked out of the building. He had seen that movie *Pump Up the Volume*. He could continue to broadcast his word to the faithful. It was up to him to expose the truth about local political corruption and the green hoax.

The next day Al smuggled an FM transmitter, broadcast antenna, a 4-channel mixer, and various cables out of the station. It was easy. He walked in dragging a large plastic deck box and told the receptionist he was there to remove a few things from his office. She even procured a dolly for his chest. He had his own netbook and tripod at home. That was everything he needed.

Once home, he put the transmitter, mixer, and netbook in the box. He rigged a piece of tape across the front of his box with the words "Ham Radio Repeater" scrawled across it in black marker. That was in case anyone happened across the box before he got it situated. "Plausible deniability," he snickered. He felt very smart.

When night fell, he set about rigging up his pirate radio station at the Grow House.

"If the FCC tracks this down, these asswipes will be blamed." It was hard not to beam with pride at this master stroke. "I'm a goddamn fucking genius." Al whispered to himself.

Wearing all black and a ski mask, he pushed a dumpster under the fire escape, closed the lid, lifted his box on top of it, and then climbed the fire escape to the roof.

Lugging the five-foot long box up the two flights of the fire escape was not easy, but hey, all in the name of Truth. He nearly collapsed at the top as he pulled the unwieldy box over the lip of the building. Huffing from exertion, he hooked the gear in the box to his tripod-based antenna. Using his flashlight and trying not to trip over Free's rooftop garden boxes, he searched until he found an electrical outlet. The laptop was hooked up to the Internet via stupid Free

Byrd's Wi-Fi, which wasn't even secured. What a moron. He placed the whole shebang behind the small brick building that housed the stairs. Once everything was set up, he scurried back down the fire escape.

From his apartment Al made sure his software was in working order. Tomorrow was going to be a good day.

***

The week was unusually hot and muggy. Both protesting factions had taken to wearing bathing suits to the Square. When the heat became insufferable, they stood in the fountain. This was not popular among the small children of Knoxville, whose parents took one look at the scraggly band and hustled their swimsuit-wearing tikes, screaming their own protests, away.

Even the cool spray of water did little to soothe their crankiness on the muggiest days. The Left's organizers were finding it harder and harder to talk their comrades back from the brink of open hostility. The Right's organizers didn't even try.

Al was so excited he hardly slept. He was up early checking and double-checking the links to his radio station. He planned to commandeer 1310 AM during his regular broadcast time. The previous evening he called a few faithful protesters who had a boom box connected to a speaker on the north end of Market Square. They checked for Al's broadcast every day and transmitted it loudly when he was on the air. He let them know he would be broadcasting live today. They were overjoyed. That would show the fascists at the station! He could hardly contain his glee.

He'd spent a lot of time looking for unsecured Wi-Fi spots. He could park in front of his neighborhood bakery café, in one of the student housing parking lots on campus, and nine houses down from his apartment. Today he parked in front of student housing and fiddled with the settings on his laptop until he was he was all set. He was one mouse click away from Truth.

Meanwhile, his faithful comrades were fiddling with their boom box and speaker on the Square. At precisely 10 a.m., an ear-shattering sound broke over the speaker, interrupting the opening strains of a pre-recorded episode of *Al and Brent in the Morning*.

Squeeeeeee click squeeeee

"Welcome to Pirate Al in the Morning, Knoxville!"

The squeal of Ted Nugent's "Stand" blared from the speaker.

I don't need nobody to hold my hand, don't need nobody, I can stand. Make it on my own in a rock 'n' roll band, kiss my American ass, I'm a Republican.

One by one, the protesters turned in the direction of the sound.

"Today we appeal to the good sense of the citizens of Knoxville. We are here to keep the lunatics from taking over, from trashing our city, from destroying the moral fiber of our society." Al's voice boomed over the Square.

The protesters of the Right nodded their heads in unison as they moved closer.

"Liberals in our town are telling us to tone down the political rhetoric. Well, to the faithful I say, it is time to TURN IT UP. Only pathetic, fetus-hating fools could believe that toning it down will somehow bring our city back from the brink of communism and illegal drugs."

"Preach it," someone in the crowd yelled.

"Good point," called another.

"I don't think name-calling is necessary," called someone from the back.

"We must expose and eliminate liberals and their free-market-fearing policies," Al continued boldly.

Half the crowd was whistling and clapping. The other half was booing.

"Do America a favor and crush liberalism! Death to the brie-eating whiners!"

The Right went wild. Their roar of agreement was met with the Left's vehement hisses and boos.

A longhaired liberal in the front of the crowd looked to his conservative counterpart and said, "I got your rhetoric right here."

With one shove, the whole horde fell into a mad brawl. Picket signs came crashing down on heads. A volley of rotten vegetables flew through the air. Otherwise peaceful protesters grappled with the opposition. Weeks of suppressed hostility finally found a blessed outlet.

Al's voice sailed out over the brouhaha. "Meet me at the Mayor's press conference on June twenty-fourth and let your voices be heard. We'll show those traitorous, Prius-driving asshats how to go home and hug a tree!"

Squaaaaaaaaack squeeeeeeeee click

A shot rang out from the crowd, and the speaker blasted to pieces. The fracas raged on amidst a shower of sparks and plastic. Bystanders screamed as they ran for cover in nearby stores and restaurants. Panhandlers stood on the sidelines cheering on the battle. The bar crowd grabbed their drinks off patio tables and made for the inside, hooting and calling from their ringside view at the windows. Cries of "Fight! Fight! Fight!" came from every direction.

In no time at all, seven squad cars surrounded Market Square. Billy clubs flying, the officers leapt into the fray to pull the battlers apart.

The protesters then turned on the police. Outraged, they taunted the officers as they hurled vegetables.

"Police brutality!"

"This is America, not Tiananmen Square!"

"Freedom of speech!"

The majority, though, high-tailed it around the corner restaurant and ran for their cars. The ones who didn't run were handcuffed and neutralized until the paddy wagons arrived. Some, however, waited for the ambulance. At least one had a ruptured eardrum from having his head held down in the spray of the fountain.

KNOXTOPIA
Plant a Garden. Change the World.

Knoxville Needs Some Nonviolent Direct Action Training

Market Square has been blissfully quiet for three whole days following a violent protest in which many were arrested. Some of you may think I'm ridiculous for offering tips on nonviolent resistance to people who are picketing *me*, but recent events downtown warrant some real talk.

You may be aware that the Right is currently protesting KUE Gardens, and the Left is counter-protesting. We won't get into the details as to why this is happening, but really, folks, there's no need for name-calling or throwing punches. I respect your right to protest, just let's be civil. And guns? Why would you bring a gun into an already volatile situation?

Nonviolence means avoiding not only external physical violence but also internal violence of spirit. You not only refuse to shoot a man, but you refuse to hate him.—Martin Luther King, Jr.

Gandhi said we need to be the change we want to see. That's what I have tried to do with my life. That's why I'm involved with KUE. I believe organizing and working together to get a message out works. Some of you are doing that to let it be known you do not like what I am doing, specifically as it relates to the mayor's overall Green Initiative.

I respect that, but there's a better way to do it if you want people to really listen.

The Golden Rule of protesting is that we must occupy the moral high ground at all times. I didn't see that happening outside KUE Gardens this week. I find it interesting that members of the Right who have taken to the streets are still bullying and overpowering like our repressive institutions have always done. They are just taking it to a personal level.

What's wrong with this picture? The hate is still there. The violence is still there. The guns are still there. They are still trying to scare us. They are co-opting our methods and continuing their violence.

And to my friends on the Left, what happened to the peacekeepers? What happened to nonviolent resistance?

Friends, whether we are protesting KUE Gardens or nature-destroying agribusiness, we need a strategy that validates alternatives, supports freedom, and creates cooperation. We need a living revolution. For real revolutionary change, we need a new culture, a new way of being. We can't get rid of repressive hierarchies if we still play domination games in our heads.

We will disagree, but the difference is in how we handle our disagreements. The moment we move into violence, we have lost. Don't just react. Offer alternatives. Create trust. Communicate your stance.

My advice to the Right: I recommend you appoint a leader and several peacekeepers. Have strategic planning meetings. What is your goal? What's the best way to accomplish it? Be focused. When hot heads prevail, the peacekeepers can swoop in and be the voice of calm. There's a way to do this, people. If you need a peacekeeper training agenda, stop by the warehouse. I'll be happy to share mine. I've had plenty of training. In fact, kNOxNUKES offers free training classes. Consider sending a representative.

To the Left: Reread *The Politics of Nonviolent Action*.

1,312 Comments

TOP COMMENTS

Garden_Guy said ...

All good points. I volunteer to help with peacekeeping from here on out. I'll be happy to run workshops or sit down with leaders of both sides to mediate.

(189 Comments <u>View</u>)

TeaBaggin4Ever said ...

I call bullshit. Don't be a wimp. If you can't take the heat, get out of the kitchen, liberal pussies.

(477 comments <u>View</u>)

GreenByNature said ...

All you Repugnicans are acting like a bunch of babies throwing a tantrum. Does baby want a bottle?

(202 Comments <u>View</u>)

<u>VIEW ALL COMMENTS</u>

« CHAPTER 9 »

PEARLY FIDGETED IN THE backseat of Sidewinder's Jeep. Acacia, his girlfriend, sat beside him in the passenger seat. They all wore dark clothes and black knit caps. It was just after 11 p.m. They had been sitting across from the entrance to the Oak Ridge Y-12 National Security Complex on Bear Creek Road since nightfall waiting for any suspicious trucks to leave the site. Passing the Army-green binoculars between them, they took turns marking down the comings and goings from the plant. Tracking the convoys that leave the nuclear weapons facility wasn't a high priority on the anti-war front anymore, but with America's hawkish military stance increasing around the world, they had a renewed vigilance. Somebody had to keep the industrial military complex accountable for their actions.

The three met at an EarthFirst! encampment in Kingston after the black coal fly ash spill into the

Emory River of Roane County. Trying to call attention to other toxic sludge ponds in the region, the activists had staged some street theater outside the Holiday Inn in Lenoir City during Erin Brockovich's press conference there. The celebrity lawyer had given Pearly a thumbs-up on her way into the hotel with her entourage.

"Remember, ladies, if anything ever goes down at these actions like raids or arrests or other violence, we should scatter." Sidewinder had a map of the Y-12 reservation open and spread across his steering wheel. "The work we're doing now isn't threatening, but it wouldn't do the revolution any good if we were all sitting in a jail cell. Better to scatter, regroup, and continue to protest another day."

"How do we do that if we're all sitting in the same car?" It was Acacia's turn with the binoculars.

Sidewinder shot her a sarcastic look. "You know what I mean. It's a good policy. Each activist needs their own get-out-of-jail plan that does not include fellow protesters. That way, you're sure to get out of jail if everyone is arrested, and all protesters could be free agents, taking responsibility for themselves."

"That seems counterintuitive," Pearly interjected. "I thought we counted on power in numbers? That's what I've always been taught at direct action training camps. If someone gets arrested, we help until they are free."

"Well, for this action, we scatter," Sidewinder said. "I don't have the means to get you out of jail if you're arrested, and this isn't a kNOxNUKES sanctioned outing, anyway."

"Just say it, Sidewinder, you've got warrants for past protests and you don't dare go within a hundred feet of a police station." Acacia gave him a tight-lipped smile.

"That's not the point. We don't need to worry about that anyway. No one's going to jail."

"I agree with you there," Pearly said. "It's quiet on the nuclear front these days, what with the so-called dismantlement in progress." Pearly wasn't going to lie. She was a little disappointed. Acacia passed her the binoculars.

"Are you kidding me?" Sidewinder turned in his seat. "This country's 'backdoor' nuclear proliferation policies are in full swing. Congress wasn't giving any money for new bomb programs, so the weaponeers revamped programs that Congress *would* fund. Shiesty bastards. They're using the Life Extension Program to remake the old bombs into something new. Y-12 is refurbishing the Trident missiles. It's more bombs under the same name."

"We know, Side. Preaching to the choir." Acaia sounded bored.

Sidewinder didn't take the hint. "The Y-12 Nuclear Plant's example of refurbishment is the equivalent to me taking my beat up old Toyota to the mechanic and getting a new Porsche in return. It is clearly not the same car, not the same nuclear weapon."

"Weren't there some shady delays on that project in the past?" Acacia took a long toke from a glass pipe packed with pot and passed it and her lighter to Pearly. When she exhaled, the smoke curled around her head.

"Yeah, they had to stop the project to develop a classified substance codenamed Fogbank," said Sidewinder. "The fuckers forgot how to make it! They were spending billions of dollars trying to recreate it. Not only that, but Fogbank is an environmental nightmare in and of itself. They use some highly flammable, toxic chemical shit to make it at Y-12. Even the scientists say it's dangerous."

"What exactly is it and how in the hell could they forget how to make it?" Pearly asked on her own exhale. She passed the paraphernalia to Sidewinder, who paused to hit the pipe.

"Pearly, don't encourage any more mansplaining, *please*."

Sidewinder gave Acacia a dirty look. "It's an extremely low-density material that looks like smoke or fog or some shit." Sidewinder stopped to cough. When it seemed like he might finally choke to death, he caught his breath and continued. "It's used to insulate the hot bomb components. I don't know. Apparently the project was mothballed during a non-proliferation phase, and people retired. Shit like that."

"Why aren't we still out here with signs and actions?" Pearly asked, aghast.

"Some of us are." Acacia said.

"Nobody tells them," Sidewinder countered. "Y-12 is busy these days. Not only is it Ground Zero for the life extension plan, but the feds are building a new bomb plant in Oak Ridge, a $3.5 billion uranium processing facility."

"We can't stay quiet about this." Pearly decided then and there that this was her new mission. That's how kNOxNUKES 2009 got started. The three devised a plan to meet in Oak Ridge to begin tracking trucks that left the facility.

"Well, let's take turns watching now." Acacia said. "You all snuggle down and rest. I'll take first watch."

***

"Guys, wake up!" It was 2:13 a.m., and Pearly was watching a convoy pull out of the complex. Sidewinder jumped in his seat. Acacia stirred, her head propped on the passenger side window. Two unmarked cars followed two military trucks out of the gates, headed for the highway.

"Quick! Quick! Follow them!" Pearly cried as she poked Acacia awake. Sidewinder started the car and pulled out onto the road.

"What? Stop it! I'm awake."

Pearly wrote furiously in the watcher's log as all four vehicles headed east toward Knoxville. "Who do we call? What do we do?" The boredom of the last few hours was replaced with near panic as they began their chase.

"Let's call the office of NukeWatcher and leave a message. That way, we've reported it, and if anything happens to us, they'll know what we were doing," said Sidewinder. "That's protocol." Acacia hit speed dial on her cell phone, and was reporting within seconds to the answering machine. "Let's report every half hour so we'll have a log of events," she said.

As they drove through Knoxville, one truck split off from the caravan at the downtown exit. The rest of the vehicles continued on down the highway. There was no question about which to follow. Without a moment's hesitation, Sidewinder took the exit. Acacia dialed the office.

"What are they doing?" he asked in astonishment. "They aren't supposed to split up."

"This isn't right," Acacia said. "What if the truck is a decoy and the other vehicles are transporting the bombs?"

"We don't even know if they're transporting bombs," said Pearly. "It could be anything."

"There are tracking and GPS devices on official transports," Sidewinder said. "Maybe the other vehicles are decoys with the tracking devices."

The truck made the next exit off the freeway and through the Knoxville tunnel, emerging on Henley Street. It made another right and then turned into the World's Fair Park. Sidewinder slowed the car to a crawl, attempting to stay out of sight. "Let's get out and follow on foot," he said.

The three parked across the street from the Convention Center and skirted the edge of the bus stop to get a better look at the truck from street level. It slowed to a stop by the Sunsphere down below. Two heavily armed men in khakis jumped out of the cab and walked to the back of truck. Another man materialized from the shadowy base of the Sunsphere and spoke with them briefly. He then headed back to the building.

The two truck drivers opened the back doors of the truck. One disappeared into the trailer while the other stood watch. The third man returned with an industrial dolly. Pearly, Sidewinder, and Acacia looked out from behind the top of the stairs. They heard some banging inside the trailer and low murmurs as the men conversed. They piled metal cylinders on the dolly. The ping of an elevator door pierced the silence as the three men pushed the load into the lift at the base of the Sunsphere.

"Holy shit! What are they doing?" Sidewinder reached for Acacia's cell phone to call the office, but Acacia darted from their hiding place and ran for the elevator door.

"Acacia!" Pearly hissed. "Come back here!" She hurried after her friend, leaving Sidewinder behind.

The doors to the elevator closed just as Pearly reached them. She watched the lighted floor numbers pause at the fourth floor before it began its way back down. When they opened again, she stepped inside. The door closed behind her.

She dug in her bag until she found her own cell phone. She dialed Free, though she was sure he was asleep. No answer. The call went to voicemail. She spoke softly into the phone. "Free, I'm at the Sunsphere. Something crazy is happening. We followed a truck from Y-12 here. They are loading cylinders of something off the truck and hauling them inside. Acacia ran in, and I'm going after her. If you get this, come meet me at the Amphitheater. I'm worried we're in over our heads. Try not be seen."

She pushed the button for the public, fourth floor. She could only hope that the truckers weren't looking at the elevator. When the elevator stopped, she stepped out into the unremarkable observation deck. Through the tinted glass that encircled the floor, the night looked especially dark. The room was illuminated only by an exit sign above a door. A sign said, "Emergency Exit Only—Alarm Will Sound."

Taking her chances, she tried the door. It was unlocked. She stepped into the stairwell. No alarm sounded. Turning, she began the ascent up the stairs in the dark. She felt her way up one flight of stairs until she felt the door to the fifth floor. She started up the next flight of stairs, counting doors until she was within sight of the eighth floor.

***

Sidewinder watched as a lone figure emerged from the stairwell. Acacia scurried toward him.

"I followed them to the fourth floor but couldn't go further. You apparently need an elevator key to get to the higher floors. Hey, where's Pearly?"

"She's in there. Didn't you see her?" Sidewinder looked worried.

"No, I took the stairs down when I heard the elevator. Dammit. It must have been her. I'll go back and get her."

At the approaching sound of a siren, Sidewinder grabbed Acacia's arm. "No. We've got to get out of here."

The two ran for the Jeep. Acacia was barely inside before Sidewinder accelerated down the block. Just as they turned the corner, a fire truck barreled over the Clinch Avenue Bridge on a routine drill, siren blasting.

***

Barely breathing, Pearly squatted low in the darkened stairwell. She could hear movement on the landing above. Mustering her courage, she raised her head for a peek. The dolly sat at the top of the stairs, empty. The three men were hauling the last of its cargo up a metal ladder into what must be an attic space at the very top of the building. One of the men handed up a cylinder to one of the two above.

"Let's get the rest. We need to hurry before we're seen," he said.

"Dude is coming up the elevators now with the last of it," a gruff voice said.

Pearly realized she had come this far without a plan. She fumbled with her bag and pulled out her cell phone. Holding it in front of her, she decided to take a picture of the men and their mysterious goods. Evidence. She needed evidence. She fumbled with the camera to turn off the flash. When she pointed the phone and pushed the camera button, the flash erupted into the darkness. Damn!

"Hey!" yelled the man at the bottom of the ladder. Pearly turned and ran down the stairs. Within seconds, she heard a pair of boots stomping down the stairs behind her. One set of footsteps. She could outrun one.

Panic seized her. All she could do was run. She lost count of the floors. She would never have time to wait at the fourth floor elevator anyway. Finally the stairs ended and she flung herself out into the night.

She skirted the building in the dark, hoping it shielded her from view even a little. The Jeep. Where was the Jeep?

She hesitated for a beat, then turned toward the Amphitheater, her heart pounding. Free would be there. She barreled across the plaza toward the man-made lake. She had no plan. She could only run from the footsteps gaining ground behind her.

A hand grabbed her by the hair and yanked hard. She jerked back violently and went down, hitting the concrete with a sickening thud. She kicked and screamed as he dragged her the remaining distance to the water. She scrambled desperately, clawing his boots, his knees. She scratched at his arms, any exposed skin.

He cursed and pulled harder.

She screeched until her face slammed into the water. She thrashed as the flood burst into her lungs, her head exploding with lights and the sound of churning water. Her throat burned and her ears pounded as she vainly lashed out at the man behind her.

He shoved her deeper underwater. He didn't move until she was still.

He stood knee-deep in the shallow pool, mesmerized by the way her hair fanned out in a halo, until the sound of approaching sirens brought him back. Panting and wet, he jumped out of the water and ran for the truck where the others waited. They peeled off in a cloud of burning rubber.

***

Asleep in his teepee, Free reached for the cell phone on the last ring. "Hello?" He wasn't completely awake. He sat up, rubbed his eyes, and checked his messages. It was Pearly. He snapped his phone shut and reached for his jeans and car keys.

There was no traffic in downtown Knoxville at three in the morning. He was at the fair site in minutes. Parking on Clinch Avenue at the bus stop, he took the steps two at a time as he approached the Sunsphere. No one seemed to be there. Looking around nervously, he tried the door. It was locked. He paused before stepping out into the open plaza, checking for any sign of disruption. Cautiously, he headed for the Amphitheater. There by the water's edge, was a cell phone. It was Pearly's. He pocketed it and kept walking.

He saw something bulky floating in the water. He recognized the hair first. There, floating face down was Pearly. Before he could reach out to her, a voice shouted, "Freeze! Hands above your head!" He hadn't even heard the police sirens.

***

Emma hadn't been to the police station in the middle of the night since Abe had snuck out to go joy-riding in her car. He was fifteen. That time she had merely picked him up. This time she called a bail bonds office and her lawyer. The wait was long and agonizing.

Detectives had taken Emma down to the morgue to identify the body before Free got out of jail. She would never be able to scrub that memory out of her mind. Beautiful Pearly, now lifeless and pale with blue lips and broken fingernails, her hair wildly knotted and eyes bulging. She had struggled. She had fought back hard. Her face was swollen as though she had been soundly beaten.

It was noon before Free was released to her custody. She took one look at him and cried. She grabbed him and pulled him into a deep hug. "I'm so sorry. I'm so sorry," she murmured. Free was still. They stood like that for several minutes. Finally, Emma's lawyer interrupted them.

"Emma, I need to be going. I'll be in touch. You keep your eye on him, now."

"Of course, thank you." She turned to Free and made him look into her eyes. His eyes were swollen and red. "Free, what happened?"

"I don't know. I got a call from her. She said something was weird. I went to find her," he choked back a sob.

"How can they think you did this?"

"I was at the scene, knee-deep in water beside her. No witnesses, Emma. There were no witnesses."

"Why was she even there?"

"I don't know, but we're going to find out. I have her phone. Maybe we can piece together what happened. We have to. If we don't, I'm going to jail for murder."

As soon as Emma got Free to the car, he pulled out Pearly's phone.

"How did you get away with her phone?" Emma asked, astonished.

"Thank God for shoddy police work," Free answered. "Mine was in my truck. They just assumed it belonged to me." As soon as he turned the phone on, it beeped with missed calls. "Two people called multiple times. The names are Sidewinder and Acacia." He hit "dial" on the last call and placed it on speaker phone. It only rang once.

"Oh god, Pearly," a man's voice said. "We were worried to death. What happened?"

"I was hoping you could tell me that," Free said anxiously.

"Who is this?"

"My name is Free. Pearly and I were seeing each other. I hope you can give me some insight into how she died."

"She died?" Free heard the phone drop and two voices talking excitedly in the background. Another voice came to the phone, a female voice.

"Hello? Hello, please, tell us what happened. We should have waited. Oh god, we should have waited."

Free told Acacia what he knew, and listened as she told him about Pearly's last night at the gates of the nuclear power plant.

"We panicked. She ran in like that. We heard sirens and we drove away. We're terrible." Speaking to her companion, she said, "Why did we run?" Acacia was crying now. Free could hear Sidewinder in the background. "We had a pact. We all knew we had to take responsibility for our own actions. Wait, how did *he* get her phone?" He sounded panicked. "Maybe he's the murderer!" The call was abruptly ended on their end.

Emma and Free started their search immediately upon getting back to Emma's house. Free sat down with Pearly's phone to write down all incoming and outgoing calls. Who was going to take care of her remains, Emma asked. Where was her family? Free wasn't sure.

"Well, we know they followed a truck from Oak Ridge to the Sunsphere. We know they were spooked. We can assume someone didn't want Pearly to know what was up there." Emma tapped off the points on her fingers. "And those two will probably disappear. Didn't she tell us once she met them at an EarthFirst encampment? They probably aren't even from here, and they probably think you are the killer."

Free sighed. "At least we know a little about what was going on. Now how do we find out the rest?"

"If somebody was willing to kill Pearly over the contents of that truck, an awful lot of money must be at stake. In all the mysteries I've ever read, the heroes have followed the money. Looks like we need to figure out what was in that truck and who paid to have it stored in the Sunsphere."

"How are we going to find out what they're doing in Y-12? All that information is classified, isn't it?"

"More than likely, but you are *not* going to prison for a murder you didn't commit. Let's get some sleep. We've been up all night. We'll start digging after we get a little rest."

***

Emma was too wired to sleep, so she hit the computer almost immediately. First she searched for kNOxNUKES. She got a good idea about what the nuclear industry had been up to in the past few years, but the national organization, NukeWatcher, hadn't been actively tracking bombs in the U.S. for quite some time. She did find out that the military was "retooling" missiles under the Life Extension Program.

She went to the EarthFirst! website, but couldn't find mention of Y-12 in recent actions, so that was a bust. She entered Pearly's name in the search engine and got about a million hits for the endangered mussel whose name she had assumed.

When Free woke up around 5 p.m., Emma was still at the computer, having only gotten up to go to the bathroom and grab a bite.

"So what have you found?"   Free looked awful.

"Not enough. Y-12 certainly keeps its work under wraps, but I've researched some of the science journalists in the area. There are some interesting theories about what's going on, but who really knows? It's not like any of them have security clearances, so it's all speculation."

"So let's back up," Free said. "Who has access to the Sunsphere? What big cheese could hide something there and hope to get away with it?"

"Well, I guess we can look into all the businesses that have offices there. We can find out who owns it, who has keys to the building, and who goes in and out." Emma ran her hand through her hair. "We know the City owns it. We know that Jackson Taurus manages it for the city. We can easily get a list of businesses."

"Then that's where we start. Let me have the computer for a while. It's your turn to go get some rest. Tomorrow during business hours we can hit the pavement downtown."

When Emma awoke early the next morning, she found Free asleep at the desk. Surrounding him were printouts of pictures of the inside of the Sunsphere and other information about Y-12. God bless the Internet. She gathered up the sheets and carried them to the kitchen, where she set about making coffee.

He'd found pictures of every floor of the structure, including a news article about the observation deck remodel. She studied them closely. Emma had to wonder how many locked doors they were going to have to navigate.

Free woke shortly after and shuffled to a stool at the kitchen island. He held his head in his hands.

"You don't look so good, friend," Emma said. She put an arm around him while she poured his coffee. He laid his head on her shoulder.

"I didn't know Pearly that well, but she was something, wasn't she?" Free sounded frail.

"She was. And we're going to find her killer. She won't die in vain. You did some good work last night. I think we should start with the kNOxNUKES office and then try to get into the Sunsphere. There's a restaurant up there. We can pretend we're interested in booking a reception. Maybe they'll take us on a tour."

"I doubt if what we're looking for will be out in the open. In her message she said they were hauling cylinders of something."

"Right, but we can case the joint and come back later to search. What comes from Y-12? Enriched uranium, right?"

Emma pawed through the photo printouts again and pulled out a picture of gloved hands holding a flat metallic disc eight or nine inches in diameter. "I guess these round discs would stack in cylinders? Argh. Where's a physicist when you need one?"

Free pulled Pearly's phone out of his pocket and absently looked through her contacts. He pulled up her camera roll as an afterthought. He sat straight up and called Emma over.

"Look! A picture."

A somewhat blurred shot filled the screen. Two men were looking down from an attic or crawl space while a third was standing beneath them lifting up a cylinder to their waiting hands. "The time stamp is right around the time of Pearly's death. This was taken minutes before she died."

Emma looked closer and rummaged through Free's printouts until she found the pictures she was looking for. She compared them to Pearly's picture. "That's the top tier of the Sunsphere. Let's print this out. These might be the killers."

It didn't take long to download and print the last few pictures from the phone, which included shots of a truck leaving Y-12, traveling down the highway, and pulling into the Sunsphere.

"I don't think anyone could haul enriched uranium in those kinds of canisters and live to tell the tale. It must be something else," said Free.

"The license plates in these pictures are too damned blurry," Emma complained. "Maybe if we can blow them up. Wait, maybe Sidewinder or Acacia got the numbers."

"They aren't answering calls now. I think they've split. Maybe they called it in to NukeWatcher. Let's keep to your original plan—kNOxNUKES and the Sunsphere."

Emma sighed. "Okay. I'll get dressed. We need to feed the chickens too."

"I'll do it, and I'll do a bit more research on who might have access to that area of the Sunsphere. Although, I think we can guess."

***

"I looked up Taurus and his business ventures on the newspaper website while you were getting dressed," Free said on the way downtown. "You were right about his Sunsphere project. He's poised to lose millions if he backs out of his development plan. It's doubly bad because he lost big on another development project just last year, according to the newspaper archives. I think he's putting all his eggs in one Sunsphere with this current project to recoup those losses. Big money equals big motivation."

"Right. It's pretty obvious he's suspect number one. Add to that the fact that he manages the site."

"The evidence does appear to be mounting."

They pulled into the kNOxNUKES office, which was housed in a rundown home just behind the main drag of the UT campus. It was locked up tight. A sign on the door read "Closed until further notice. Should you need assistance, please contact our national hotline." Free typed the contact number on the door into his phone. He handed it to Emma. "Maybe you should call. My name might be on their radar by now. I have no idea what the news is reporting about Pearly's death."

Emma did as he directed and handed him his phone back. "The recorded message said it might be a while before they get back to us. I guess we'll head to the World's Fair Park now."

They made the short drive from the University to downtown and parked at the Knoxville Museum of Art, just a couple of blocks from the Sunsphere.

"I hear the Observation Deck is open to the public now. We shouldn't have any trouble getting that far." Free said. "Even if we can, let's not take the elevator to the top. It might open into offices, and we'll be noticed. We may need key cards for offices above the Observation Deck." The morning sun glinted off the giant golden sphere, causing them to squint as they got nearer. They took the stairs to the Sunsphere elevator. Soon they were looking at a building directory on the fourth floor.

"Well, the bar on the fifth floor doesn't open until four. I wonder how easy it's going to be to get around. Looks like the catering business is on the sixth floor. Business offices on the sixth, seventh, and eighth. Look! Taurus Enterprises has an office on the seventh floor."

"And we need to get to the eighth," Emma added.

They jumped as the elevator opened, A delivery man with a Big R Cola cap emerged with a clipboard. Emma and Free feigned interest in the directory marquee as he walked up behind them.

"Do you see Jackson Taurus on there anywhere?" he asked.

"Seventh floor, buddy," Free answered after casually running his finger down the listing.

"Thanks. Oh wait. This manifest says he'll meet me on the eighth floor." He whistled as he waited for the elevator again. When it seemed to take too long, he disappeared through a door to the stairwell.

"So, not locked." Free observed. "Let's give him a head start and then we'll follow."

After a few minutes they cautiously opened the door to the stairs and started up. At the eighth floor door they paused. "You first," Emma said as she gently pushed Free to the door. He opened it a crack and peeked through. Voices filtered through the door.

"Yes. Be sure to have these out of here by five o'clock on June twenty-fourth. Just so we're clear: Deliver the new soda fountain cylinders here and pick up these old ones to be delivered to another location. You'll find the cylinders under a tarp at the top of the ladder in the stairwell. Bring someone to help you haul them. Just drop the new cylinders there in the corner."

A familiar voice—Jackson Taurus.

"Yes, sir. Do you need us to install the new CO_2 cylinders on your soda fountains?"

"No, these are spare inventory. Festivities start at seven, so you need to be clear of here. There will be a truck waiting for you at this address. Just help them load up the cylinders and you're done. Have your company invoice me."

"Sir, we'll be happy to get these out of here before the festival. We can leave them at our dock and deliver them right on time."

"No. That won't be necessary. Just do as I say."

"Yes, sir. I need you to sign here. And initial here. Are these goods fragile, liquid, perishable, or potentially hazardous?"

"No, I told you. They're vintage soda fountain cylinders. You're delivering them to a collector."

"Fine, sir. Initial here. We'll take care of it for you."

"All right. We're finished here."

Free gently closed the door and hustled Emma down the stairs. "Go. Go. Go," he whispered urgently. Not sure if Taurus was heading for the stairs or the elevator, they ran down the steps as quickly and quietly as they could. They ducked in the Observation Deck.

"Looks to me like Taurus is our man. We just have to be here when the cylinders are moved to see exactly where they are going. Then we'll have our answers." Emma hit the elevator button. "Let's get out of here."

When the door opened, Jackson Taurus and the deliveryman stood in front of them.

"Ms. Goode. What a happy coincidence. I was just going to call you this afternoon. Mr. Byrd." He nodded coolly in Free's direction. "What in the world brings you here?"

"An appointment with a caterer," she replied stiffly. Seeing no other option, Emma and Free stepped into the elevator.

"Yes, well." He straightened his silk tie, jeweled pinky finger extended. "We are organizing a press conference for the mayor during the International Festival. He's announcing the Green Initiative. You and your friend need to be there. Semi-formal. Can you handle that? Call my office for details."

"I am aware of the press conference," Emma said.

"Then be there."

The door opened onto the street level, and Free and the Big R driver walked out. Taurus grabbed Emma's shoulder from behind as she took a step to leave.

"That gives you a very short time to walk away from your Sunsphere project. If it isn't done by the festival, I'll make my own announcement to the press right after I drop your sons' tapes in the mail."

Emma jerked out of his grasp and stomped out of the elevator. Taurus, adjusting his diamond cuff links, headed for the parking garage.

***

"What would Taurus steal from Y-12 and hide in the Sunsphere?" They had returned home, and Emma was back at the computer. Pulled up on the screen was a picture of cylinders identical to the ones in Pearly's photo. Some disgruntled former employee had smuggled the picture out of Y-12's Highly Enriched Uranium Materials Facility. She tapped her finger on her computer mouse as she thought. "It can't be radioactive. Aren't those stored in thick lead containers?"

"I'm not sure we need to know what it is. It came from Y-12 under the darkness of night and it is going out under false pretenses. It's bad." Free propped himself against the desk where Emma worked.

"What exactly do they do at Y-12?"

"Lots of stuff. They refurbish and decommission warheads for one. They manufacture a component codenamed Fogbank for the Trident missiles. They're also responsible for the maintenance and production of all uranium parts for every nuclear weapon in the United States arsenal. And as the

HEUM name implies, they do a lot with enriched uranium."

"But isn't all that stuff closely guarded?"

"Well, the economy *has* tanked. People will do just about anything for money. Hey, remember those protestors who cut the fence and vandalized the HEUM not long ago? The lax security was a national scandal. I heard security turned off the alarms because wildlife kept setting it off. They've beefed up security since then, but these tanks could have been moved to a less secure area on the Oak Ridge reservation then, and are just being hauled out. Maybe they saw their moment and took it."

"I think we can safely say it's some dangerous material on its way to some unscrupulous person for an insane amount of money. And guess who needs an insane amount of money right now? Our friend Jackson Taurus. Okay, let's talk terrorism. Who is in the market for contraband from a nuclear reservation?"

"It could be anybody from homegrown to international terrorists or even nations." Free scratched his stubbly face as he thought. "OK, well ... China is accelerating their plans for a nuclear reactor. They're going to need enriched uranium to transform into fuel. As if Fukushima wasn't enough of a cautionary tale. But they would need an obscene amount of uranium. A truckload wouldn't make a dent."

Emma snapped her fingers impatiently. "Nations. Give me the names of nations."

"There are five recognized nuclear weapons states: China, France, Russia, England, and America. Four more countries have acquired them without the consent of the Non-Proliferation Treaty: India, Pakistan, North Korea, and Israel, I believe."

Emma had never been so glad for Free's near-encyclopedic knowledge of peace and social justice issues. "We know it's not an international conspiracy centered in Knoxville, obviously, but why Knoxville? Why now?"

The realization dawned on both of them at the same time. Eyes wide, they exclaimed together, "The International Festival!"

"Could Taurus be storing the cylinders for pickup during the festival? There are going to be dozens of international scholars there." Emma's fingers flew over the keyboard as she pulled up a list of keynote speakers. "Oh, no. Look, Free."

Free read aloud over Emma's shoulder. "A speaker from Israel. One from Pakistan. Another from India. This reads like a who's who of bad boy nuclear manufacturers. Any one of them could be here for that stuff."

"So Taurus is using the festival as a smokescreen. People will be all over the World's Fair site, and a crazy amount of delivery people will be at the scene servicing the festival. Anyone could just waltz in and carry out canisters, and nobody would think anything was amiss."

"Except for Pearly. And she died for it."

KNOXTOPIA
Plant a Garden. Change the World.

Friends, my heart is broken. Our dear friend and my lover Pearly Mussel has died. She was murdered last night at the World's Fair Park, drowned in the man-made lake. My last contact from her was a phone message in which she told me she was tracking a suspicious shipment of canisters from Oak Ridge to downtown Knoxville. She asked me to come get her, and when I arrived—I'm sorry. I don't know how many times I can say it. It's so hard to write the words.

Pearly, whose given name was Tiffany Sims, inspired us all with her inclusive spirituality. She didn't care what God you worshiped. To her, every living entity was a gift. She truly was blind to our differences—religion, color, sex, orientation, whatever. Her love knew no bounds and she never met a stranger.

If Pearly touched your life in any way, please consider honoring her through right actions. Projects dear to her heart were kNOxNUKES, United Pagans Group, and of course KUE Gardens. Volunteering, donations, and such would be a fitting tribute. Even just taking a moment to consciously respect other living things ... well, she would love that. Dance in a meadow. Snuggle a puppy. Write a letter to your Congressman. All of these would give Pearly's spirit a stupendous sendoff.

Emma sleeps while I scour the Internet for clues as to what could have happened to her. When morning breaks we will begin our search. If any of you know anything about Pearly's last day, please let us know.

506 Comments

TOP COMMENTS

GoodeAbe said ...

I am shocked and sorry to hear this. My sincerest condolences.

(109 comments View)

GreenByNature said ...

So sorry for your loss.

(45 Comments View)

VIEW ALL COMMENTS

« CHAPTER 10 »

THE REVEREND BUFORD GUNN had the *Metro Gnome* spread out before him on Vergie Dell's dining room table. Open to the Events section, he moved his index finger down the listings, his lips moving as he read to himself.

"Aha! Here's one: *Gay and Lesbian Open Mic Night. Wednesday, seven p.m., The Kaleidoscope, Kingston Pike.* I say we show up with signs that say 'God Abhors You' and one of those rainbow flags with a black X through it. Sound good?"

The Reverend's motley group murmured in assent. Vergie, the Reverend, and two other men sat around the table at an elite meeting of God's Warriors, a secret faction of the Fellowship of Christian Warriors. They needed a place to meet, so Vergie volunteered her home. This was Jay's week on the road.

"How 'bout 'God made Adam and Eve, Not Adam and Steve?'" Rowdy Snyder, who Vergie believed was not quite right, snickered. "Or 'God Hates Fags.'"

"No, we'd have to make new signs, Rowdy," The Reverend turned back to the listings. Rowdy's thin, wiry shoulders slumped under his plaid cotton shirt. The sleeves were ripped out at the shoulders, revealing a tattoo of a snarling red bobcat, the Central High School mascot.

"The Steve one's a classic, though," the Reverend added. Rowdy perked up.

Orville, who manned the door at the North Mercury meeting, took notes. He wrote in code so that the secret goings on of the group could not easily be deciphered, he told Vergie proudly before the meeting. He looked up from his squiggles.

"Are you sure we want to tangle with them feminazis? They're pretty tough. And there will be a gang of them in a bar drinking."

"Good point," said the Reverend. He continued his newspaper search. "Here's one. *Weekly Peace Vigil at Y-12.* Why do those commie peaceniks have to besmirch the good name of our military industrial complex with their stupid sit-ins? Don't they know the military keeps us safe? God knows who would run over us if we didn't have a stockpile of bombs to hide behind."

"Those towel heads would, no question," said Rowdy.

"We're Americans. We don't hide behind anything," said Orville.

"Amen, brother." Rowdy nodded his shaven head and grinned, revealing two missing teeth. "What do they do at Y-12 anyway?"

The Reverend cleared his throat pretentiously. "They do something with uranium and build triggers or something for nuclear warheads. At least, some part of a trigger. See, Americans are smart. They don't build the whole bomb in one place. They make essential parts all over the country and ship them all over the place."

"'No Peace for Terrorists' is a good slogan for a sign. Or 'We Gave Peace a Chance, We Got 9-11.' I've always wanted to carry those kinds of signs." Rowdy was getting excited.

"Those are good ones, Rowdy," Orville was writing vigorously. "Let me write those down."

"No offense, Reverend," Vergie began. "I see the need for swift action against the Gays' agenda and those anti-war nuts, but I have a real and pressing need right here in my neighborhood that needs tending."

Three pairs of eyes turned to her. "Witches are consorting in my next-door neighbor's yard. I have Internet evidence that a vast pagan conspiracy is growing up in this town, and it's liable to swallow our children if we don't act fast."

"Aren't you just inspired, Miss Vergie. Looky here. We have just the thing," the Reverend said excitedly. "*Sharing our Pagan Roots, International Festival, World's Fair Pavilion. June twenty-fourth*. Gentlemen ... and lady, I think we've found our target."

"Hey, I think we still have some of those 'Suffer Not a Witch to Live' signs from last month," Orville said. "I think we might have a couple 'Thou Shalt Have No Other God Before Me' banners, too."

"Yeah, yeah." Rowdy was almost jumping up and down. "Let's throw in a 'Repent or Perish.' I was just doing reconnaissance on them a few weeks ago. There's dissent in the ranks. They'll be easy to bust up."

"Fine. We're decided then," said the Reverend. "We can meet at the Convention Center and proceed from there."

Vergie smiled triumphantly. "Want to see where the witches congregate next door?"

The men looked at her expectantly.

"Come on," she rose from the table and headed for the stairs. "I have binoculars."

***

When Morticia started the phone tree to tell area pagans about Pearly's death, people naturally wanted to gather. Morticia instructed them to show up at the Concord Park gazebo, the site of many past rituals with their fallen sister. A crowd was forming now, and an impromptu memorial altar was developing on the steps. Among the offerings were candles, flowers, Irish whiskey, deity statues, and pictures of Earth goddesses.

Groups of people sat on the lawn, comforting each other and remembering Pearly with fondness.

"Who could have done this?"

"Why Pearly? She was a gentle soul."

"I have my suspicions," said Morticia. She was wearing all black today. The net of her witch hat was pulled over her face.

"Who?" Several voices asked in alarm.

"She and I were having coffee not too long ago at the bookstore café. One of those Fellowship people was spying on us. That Rowdy one."

Startled exclamations broke out among the crowd.

"You think he murdered her?"

"How could they do that?"

"They're always trying to sabotage our public rituals. They've picketed us and bullied us for a long time. This is the next logical step in their sick minds," Morticia's voice was getting louder in order to carry to the outer groups.

"Omigods, we've got to tell the police."

"Forget the police. I say we take this into our own hands," said Morticia. "We take care of our own."

Night Crow stepped up beside Morticia. "Of course there will have to be a ritual at the next full moon if the killer isn't caught. In the meantime, we can each devise a spell for discovery. Get together between now and the International Festival to prepare them. You can send them with us, and we'll activate them."

"So you're going to the International Festival?" Morticia asked.

"I am now. I didn't think I would, but now I see I must. After all, didn't you say Pearly desired us to be there? Gods bless her soul."

Spyder stood. "Then I shall go as well. Everyone be sure to freeze the names of the Fellowship in ice when you get home. That will stop them in their tracks. The grove and I will summon a demon among them if you like. Just say the word."

Night Crow sniffed. "You and your demons. We don't need another one loose in the community. Remember last Samhain?"

Spyder sputtered and opened his mouth to comment, but Morticia jumped in. "Then it's settled. We gather in groups to devise and strengthen our spells. We send them to the festival with Night Crow and Spyder, who will activate them at the site of Pearly's death. Choose your groups and let's get to planning."

The pagans nodded in agreement and gathered around to get started.

« CHAPTER 11 »

EMMA COULD NO LONGER put off the inevitable. It was time to talk to her sons. Rather than call them individually, she decided to talk to them via an Internet conference call, the closest she could come to a family meeting.

Her heart swelled as their faces materialized on her laptop screen. Her boys.

"Mom, hi!" Abe appeared to be sitting on the black futon in his apartment. His brown hair dusted the collar of his Greenpeace tee shirt. He pulled his boxer pup into view and waved its paw at the screen. "Sluggo says hi."

"Hello, family," said Edward from his Las Vegas office. He looked smart in his black business suit.

"Boys, I'm so glad I could get you both together. There's something I need to talk to you about."

"What, no small talk?" Edward looked concerned as he pulled closer to his computer monitor and put on his headphones.

"There will be time for small talk. I just need to get something off my chest."

"Sure, Mom. Go on." Abe set the dog down out of view.

"I don't know how to prepare you for this, so I'm just going to tell you. Your dad was having an affair when he died."

The boys were silent as they looked at each other on screen.

"I didn't tell you because I was hurt and ashamed and I didn't want you to feel the same way. I'm sorry I kept it from you."

"Why are you telling us now?" Edward had lowered his voice.

"Because I'm trying to put a warehouse farm project together here in town, and people opposed to it are digging up all the dirt on me that they can find. One especially nice man is attempting to blackmail me by threatening to tell you boys about your father's indiscretion."

Abe fidgeted a bit. "Mom, we already knew," he said softly.

Emma sat back in disbelief. "You knew?"

"Well, we suspected. All the signs were there, and Ed walked in on Dad and his assistant once."

Edward nodded. "How did you find out, Mom?"

Emma sighed heavily. "This same fellow who threatened me was married to your father's assistant. He found a tape in her office of them together. He sent it to me anonymously after your father died."

"The bastard!" Abe blurted. "What's his name?"

Edward shook his head in disbelief. "Mom, I'm so sorry you've carried this burden all this time. We didn't want to say anything to you for fear we'd break your heart."

"Boys, I'm only telling you his name so you can be on the alert for a package from him. I want no retaliation from either of you. I decided the best way to handle this was to defuse it. His name is Jackson Taurus. His business is Taurus Enterprises. Listen, should you get this package, I want you to promise me you'll destroy it without watching it. Your father was a good man in so many ways. I don't want those images to stain your memories of him." Emma paused to wipe the tears, unable to continue.

"Mom, we came to terms with this a long time ago," said Edward. "He was flawed, but we still love him."

Emma burst into tears, no longer able to hold them back.

"It's okay, Mom. Don't cry," Abe seemed close to tears himself. Seeing this, Emma wiped her face with the back of her hand and smiled.

"Okay. Okay," she snuffled. "Crazy things are going on here. This Taurus guy, he says your dad was into all kinds of backroom dealings, that he took bribes and greenwashed reports. It's just been a lot to deal with."

"Do you need me to come home to help you? I can get to the bottom of things pretty fast." Emma had no doubt that her attorney son could do just that.

"Thanks, honey, but I don't think it's that dire yet. I'll be sure to call you if it gets to that point."

"Mom, do you believe Dad could have taken bribes?" Abe sounded uncertain.

"There was a time when I would have said unequivocally no, but I just don't know anymore. I never thought he could have been unfaithful, either."

"It just doesn't sound like him. Maybe someone was holding something over his head," said Edward.

"I don't know, boys. I guess we can't know now."

When Emma broke the connection a half hour later, she felt like an enormous weight had been lifted from her shoulders.

"What did I ever do to deserve such wonderful sons?" she asked herself. Speaking to the air, she said, "That's one true thing we did together, David, in spite of the rest."

***

Picking out a dress suitable for surveillance and the Mayor's press conference was tricky. Emma needed something dressy and easy to get around in. She also didn't need bright colors signaling her whereabouts to the mysterious deliverymen. She finally settled on a black sleeveless A-line dress with a sheer slate-gray overcoat.

She almost tripped over Detective Green as she hurried out the door.

"Oh! Detective. I'm sorry."

"Mrs. Goode." He tipped his hat.

"Excuse me. I have some business to attend to before the mayor's press conference tonight. I really must be going." She eased around him.

"I just have a couple of questions for you, ma'am."

"Can we reschedule?" She headed for her car.

"This won't take long." Detective Green pulled his notebook and a pen out of his coat pocket. "Where were you on the night of Tiffany Sims' murder, Mrs. Goode?"

Startled, Emma stopped short and turned around.

"I was here," she said slowly.

"Is there anyone who can corroborate that?" Detective Green was taking notes.

"Free Byrd, but I don't suppose that does me a lot of good?"

"No ma'am." He looked up. "What time did you last see Mr. Byrd on that night?"

"We fed the animals, tended the garden, had dinner together, and he headed out to his teepee around midnight. I went to bed shortly thereafter. Before you ask, he told me the next day that Pearly, I mean, *Tiffany* called him a couple of hours later for a ride home. Something was going on, and she was scared. Free went to pick her up and found her body."

"Do you know what might have scared her?"

Emma hesitated for a moment, seemed to make a decision, and said, "She was involved with an activist group that tracked shipments to and from Oak Ridge. She was attending an action the night she died. They tracked a truck to the World's Fair Park."

"And you know this how?" The detective was scribbling furiously.

"I'll tell you everything I know soon. I have your card. Please, I really must be going."

He waved her on. "I'm going to hold you to that. Expect to see me if I don't hear from you soon."

"Thank you." She headed for her car. Before she climbed in, she looked back at the officer. "Has anyone claimed her?"

"Yes, her parents made arrangements to pick up the body yesterday. She's on her way up north for burial."

"Thank goodness. With that, Emma drove away, leaving the detective on her stoop.

***

MEDIA ADVISORY

For Immediate Release

Contact: Jerod Warner, Mayor's Office

From "Scruffy City" to Green City: Mayor to Unveil Environmental Makeover

WHAT: A press conference to announce the city's Green Initiative, specifically the creation of the new Bureau of Sustainability. Departments within the bureau will include Green Transportation, the Clean Water Project, the Clean Air Project, Recycling and Compost Services, Sustainable Planning and Buildings, the Renewable and Efficient Energy Group, and the City Farm Initiative.

WHEN: June 24, 7:30 p.m.

WHERE: Amphitheater, World's Fair Park. Parking is free.

WHO: Mayor Joe Early and the Green Initiative Committee

WHY: The City of Knoxville is working to become a leader in Green City planning and implementation. This is but the first step in the Mayor's plan to drastically improve the lives of our citizens and repair the environmental degradation in the region. The Green Initiative is slated to create hundreds of area jobs and improve the health and well-being of all Knoxvillians. A question and answer period will follow the announcement.

« CHAPTER 12 »

MORTICIA, NIGHT CROW, and Spyder set up their booth early the morning of the International Festival. After pushing two display tents together, they positioned their long folding tables and chairs. Morticia hung batik tapestries on the tent walls and spread them as tablecloths. Spyder set up a round antique table in one corner for Night Crow's rune readings. All were painfully aware of Pearly's absence.

"Should we call in another tarot card reader?" Morticia asked.

"I can alternate rune and card readings," said Night Crow. "I'll just ask which they prefer before we start. Now where are my cards?" She pawed through her large, tie-dyed shoulder bag. At once Morticia and Spyder located their own decks and shoved them under her nose. "Put those away. Here mine are." She pulled out three decks of her own and laid them on the table.

"Gods, I miss her," Morticia spread an antique doily over the round table and set a black iron candelabra to one side.

"No worries, child," Spyder said in a low tone. "We will out her murderer today."

Morticia looked to a cardboard box sitting on a long table, then to the shrubbery beside the plaza. Rowdy's ball cap could just be seen peeking up over the privet. She could only assume Rowdy was under it.

"As soon as Julianna gets here we can activate our spells," Spyder said. Julianna was the Eastern European student who procured the booth for the pagans. Her contribution to the festival was a pictorial history of the Romany tribe of her homeland. "She'll need some help arranging her photos and display first, though. And I need to set up my laptop for astrology profiles."

"I've crafted a sublime itch powder," Night Crow bragged. "The coven helped me charge it. I added in a bit of the pox as well."

"Is it targeted to the murderer?" asked Spyder.

"No, but it will cause those bastards in the Fellowship a lot of grief," she replied.

"Well, my spell is a truth spell for the murderer. He will confess," said Morticia. "It's all set. I gathered nine solitary pagans together to help me charge it. I just have to blow my truth powder toward the East. Spyder, what have you got?"

"I'll pour my Gaia potion on the ground to enlist the aid of the Earth Mother in our endeavor. The grove helped me craft it and charge it. I expect the power of nature to intervene in our quest for the murderer. Then I'll set up my mini cauldron behind the table. I'll write 'Pearly's Murderer' on a slip of paper and boil it in saltwater. After the water has boiled out, the murderer will return to the scene of the crime. We just have to wait, and he'll come to us."

"Oh, very hoodoo," Night Crow said approvingly. "Here's Julianna now."

They set about arranging photos and laying out information. Julianna hung pictures of her gypsy ancestors and created an antique tarot card display. She was dressed for the part in a flowing red skirt and head scarf. Her antique silver jewelry glinted in the morning sun. Crow and Spyder set up a display about the history of the Craft in America. They cooed and reminisced as they hung pictures of shared rituals and gatherings past on the canvas walls.

The four stepped back to admire their handiwork.

"Do you think people will think we're proselytizing?" Morticia asked.

"Well, if they do, we'll tell them we're not," Spyder said. "This is information for the sake of education and tolerance, not to create a horde of baby witches. Now, let's activate our spells as quietly as we can."

After acquiring their materials, they moved to a grassy area directly behind the booth. They held hands, closed their eyes, and seemed to fall into a deep meditative state. After a few moments, Spyder stepped to the middle of their small circle. He removed the lid of a small vial and poured the contents on the ground.

"Gaia, we call thee," he whispered. Next he reached under the tent flap and placed a tiny black cauldron on a camp stove just inside the booth. Inside the cauldron he poured water from a thermos. He pulled a salt packet and his pre-written slip of paper out of his jeans pocket and added them to the water. He turned on the stove and stepped back.

At that point Morticia stepped into the center, faced east, and poured a powder from her own vial into her hand. She blew it into the air and stepped back.

Night Crow took her turn next. She walked around the area shaking an herbal preparation out of a salt shaker. She was sure to saturate the direction of the last Rowdy sighting.

***

Rowdy practically fell out of the hedge he was occupying. He scrambled to the others who were putting the finishing touches on their signs and stuffing miniature New Testaments into their large pockets.

"Leave the box of Bibles under this here bush. After we've given away what we have, we can get more," said Reverend Gunn.

"Rev! Rev!"

Startled, the Reverend watched Rowdy's frantic approach.

"They're casting their devil spells!" Rowdy hissed. "That old one threw some kind of powder right at me." He absently scratched his arm.

"God's armor is upon us," the Reverend said. "Nothing they do can harm us."

Vergie looked up from her sign at Rowdy. "You don't look so good."

"I don't feel so good." He rubbed the back of his neck.

"Well, the power of Jesus will heal you in the doing of His work," the Reverend said. "Let's set up in front of their booth now."

"I don't know, Rev," Orville said. "If they're casting their devil spells—"

The Reverend stepped up close to Orville and stared him deep in the eyes. He placed his right hand on Orville's forehead. "*Fear thou not; for I am with thee: be not dismayed; for I am thy God: I will strengthen thee; yea, I will help thee; yea, I will uphold thee with the right hand of my righteousness."*

Vergie raised one hand to the heavens and intoned, *"He shall cover thee with his feathers, and under his wings shalt thou trust: his truth shall be thy shield and buckler. Thou shalt not be afraid for the terror by night; nor for the arrow that flieth by day; Nor for the—"*

The Reverend cleared his throat loudly. "Yes, well. Let's be about our business. Rowdy, there's your sign."

"Aw. I wanted 'Suffer Not a Witch to Live' not 'Repent or Perish.'" He eyed Orville jealously.

"Here, take it," Orville said, handing him the sign. "I don't think it's a good idea to be carrying this since that one got murdered last week. Plus it's like having a big ole bulls-eye between your eyes in front of them."

Rowdy eagerly traded signs. "So what are we doing?"

"Check your guns," the Reverend said. "We don't want to use them, but we'll have them if we need them."

All four of them pulled a concealed weapon out of various pockets—and in Vergie's case, her purse—checking them for readiness, and putting them away.

"Don't engage them," the Reverend warned. "We're just going to stand a good distance from them with our signs handing out Bibles."

"Can we make faces at them?" Rowdy asked.

"No."

"Can we holler at them?" Again, Rowdy.

"No."

"Can we stare at them righteously?"

"Rowdy." The Reverend was getting aggravated. "Well, okay. Stare at them righteously. But don't start anything with them."

Rowdy grinned, then scratched his knee.

They stepped through the bushes and skirted the pagan tent. Stopping fifty feet from the front of the booth, they nonchalantly turned around, all the while avoiding eye contact with the witches, except for Rowdy who was staring a hole through them.

The witches eyed them warily.

"Well, here they are," said Morticia.

Night Crow grinned right at Rowdy. "So they are," she said. When she waved at Rowdy, he jumped.

***

It was easy to tell the difference between the Left and the Right as they congregated at the World's

Fair Site. The majority of the Left wore jeans and printed tees with Birkenstock or Teva footwear. Some of the women wore long flowing skirts and flip flops. The men of the Right wore slacks and button-down shirts. The women were attired in business casual or Mom gear—pleated shorts, sleeveless cotton shirts, sneakers, and visors.

They all descended on the Amphitheater at approximately the same time to cheer or jeer the mayor's announcements.

Al Scheeder was dressed to the nines in a three-piece suit and tie. You never know when the TV cameras might come for your opinion, he thought. Better to be prepared. He was walking among the crowd, shaking hands and chatting amicably with the button-downs and Moms. He studiously avoided the jeans and skirts. Plenty of button-downs patted him on the back and congratulated him. He felt like a damned celebrity.

"So, Al, what do you make of all this green talk? This city has lost its mind," one admirer said, as he pumped Al's arm.

"Damn crying shame," Al responded. "This is a smokescreen for something. You can be double damn sure Big Joe doesn't do anything without some kind of kickback for himself."

"He's got these hippies brainwashed."

"Indeed he does. I wonder how they'll feel when his true colors shine through. Big Joe Early is the biggest crook the South has ever seen."

Every conversation was some variation of the theme. Big Joe was the Big Bad Wolf. The rest of the city was the Little Pigs. They had to think of some way to do him in before he blew their houses down.

***

The afternoon wore on. All day people lined up for Night Crow's tarot and rune readings with a side of Spyder's astrological profiles. People seemed as anxious for readings as they were to stay well away from the religious protestors. The Fellowship inched closer and closer throughout the day as Spyder discussed pagan spirituality with interested festival goers. Rowdy was practically in the tent at one point trying to look over Night Crow's shoulder as she read the runes. He shook his sign at her clients from behind her back. When she pulled out a salt shaker and threw a pinch of its content over her shoulder, he turned and ran the other way. He always inched back, leering and shaking his sign. This went on for the rest of the day.

Several times the park security approached the Fellowship for aggressively giving away Bibles. One scantily clad passerby complained Vergie threw a New Testament at her while yelling verses about sinners. When security confronted the Fellowship, they themselves walked away with enough Bibles to open a bookstore.

Spyder's cauldron had boiled dry. What time he wasn't talking to people at the booth was spent scanning the crowd for the possible killer. They weren't far from the scene of Pearly's murder. He was positive the killer would come back. He also watched nature for any signs of disturbance like bird flocks or sudden bursts of wind. He knew Mother Gaia would assist them.

When Morticia walked up behind Rowdy and cleared her throat, he wheeled around and hit her with his sign.

"Dude!" she howled.

"You skeered me!" Rowdy replied defensively.

"I have one question for you, asswipe. Did you kill Pearly Mussel?"

"You mean that Tiffany girl?"

"Yes."

"No, I did not."

Morticia squinted her eyes and looked closely at Rowdy's aura. By golly, he was telling the truth.

"Huh. Hey, you don't look so good."

"People keep telling me that."

The rest of the Fellowship turned away and tried to avoid eye contact when they saw Morticia approaching. She moved in close so that they had no option but to look at her.

"Did any of you kill Pearly Mussel?"

"You mean that Tiffany girl?" Vergie asked.

"Yes."

"NO!" The Reverend looked shocked at the idea.

"Of course not," Orville said as he lowered his sign.

Vergie looked Morticia up and down critically. *"Whoever takes a life shall surely be put to death."*

"Is that a no?" Morticia crossed her arms and eyed Vergie suspiciously.

"I'm standing here, ain't I? Yes, that is a no."

Morticia rolled her eyes and walked away. They were telling the truth. Before she got back to the tent, a tiny New Testament hit her square between the shoulders.

"Ow!"

"Vergie, that was the last Bible," the Reverend said tiredly.

"Should I go get more?" Vergie asked.

"I *told* you they thought we killed that girl!" Orville said under his breath.

The Reverend gasped. "How could they suspect us of murder? We're God-fearing folk! I've worked hard to create a godly reputation in this town."

With that, Orville and Vergie watched as the Reverend laid down his sign and headed in Spyder's direction.

"Sir, it's time we had a man to man discussion," the Reverend said as he pushed his way to the front of the booth. "I did not kill your friend."

"Good to know," Spyder replied. "Who did?"

"I'm sure I can't tell you, but I know how we will find out. I'll ask the Lord to deliver him to our hands."

"Thank you."

The Reverend hustled back to the group. "We need to pray that that girl's killer is found. Get Rowdy over here for a prayer meeting."

Much later, when the voice over the intercom announced the mayor's press conference, everyone but Julianna, who stayed to watch the booth, made their way to the Amphitheater.

« CHAPTER 13 »

EMMA PARKED HER CAR AT THE hotel across from the Sunsphere and waited for Free at the Clinch Avenue exit. The place was already packed with International Festival goers. As planned, Free arrived on foot at 5 p.m.

"My truck is parked on the plaza by the Sunsphere," he said. "We should be able to follow the delivery truck out undetected."

"What's the plan? Are we just going to wait for the Big R truck?"

"Works for me."

They walked to the plaza and piled into the truck's cab to wait.

"That Detective Green came back today. He asked me where I was when Pearly died."

"I'm surprised it took them this long to question you." Free shaded his eyes against the sun and looked both ways for the Big R truck. He was wearing dress slacks and a pink pin-striped dress shirt instead of his usual jeans and tee. Emma noted the suit coat neatly spread out between them. He looked nice.

"Maybe we should just tell them what we know. I'm not sure we should be sitting on this information." Emma fidgeted with the hem of her jacket.

"Let's see where this stuff is going. We can call the police from the pickup point. If they catch these guys with the goods, we're off the hook. The least we can do is get them a truck make and model or even a plate number. Look, here he comes." Free pointed to a Big R delivery truck slowly navigating the busy plaza. The truck pulled up close to the Sunsphere elevator. Two men got out and started hauling CO_2 cylinders for fountain drink machines out of the back. Emma and Free looked around nonchalantly, trying not to stare.

"That's the same guy we saw on the fourth floor," Emma said as the deliverymen hauled the tanks to the elevator.

"Yep. Right on time, too."

Emma took her phone, a pen, and Detective Green's card out of her purse. She carefully wrote the license plate number of the Big R truck on the back of the card and placed them all in her jacket pocket.

It was at least half an hour before the deliverymen came back down with Taurus' stolen goods. The tarnished tanks did indeed look like some kind of vintage collector's item. Emma used her phone to take a picture of the men as they loaded them in the back of the truck. In time they slammed down the roll-up door and climbed into the cab.

Free gave them a good head start before starting his truck and proceeding slowly. The Big R truck stopped several times for pedestrians before pulling out onto the road. Once on the main road, it went west with Free following cautiously.

"Do you ever wonder about that tarot reading Pearly gave us that night at your house?" Free asked.

"No, I haven't given it any more thought. What did she say? Victory would be ours after conflict? I sure hope she's right."

"Think about it, Emma. She said when she read the cards, two cards signify actual death in a reading for her. Those were the two cards you picked up off the floor—the Four of Swords and Death. They must have fallen out of her bag when she dropped it. Now Pearly's dead."

"How do you remember that?"

"You should have seen her face when I handed her those cards back. It's hard to forget. She also told us about an unscrupulous businessman and someone working in the shadows with him."

"We know one is Taurus."

"Right. Who's the one in the shadows?"

"I hope we'll know after tonight."

"She made it sound like more than just a business deal between two people. Didn't she use the term 'puppet master?'"

Emma looked at Free curiously. "I think so. Why?"

"She called that Devil card the Great Puppet Master." Free scratched the stubble on his chin as he drove. "God, that was a terrible reading. Why did we move forward on this?" Free's laugh was a nervous bark.

"I think everything was already set in motion, truth be told. It would have been hard to back away."

"Yeah, but none of this was worth Pearly's life."

Emma reached for Free's hand. "No, it wasn't. I know this is hard. I'm sorry."

Free gave her a weak smile. "Thanks."

They drove in silence behind the truck as it made its way west down Kingston Pike. Free pulled his hand back and placed it on the steering wheel.

"Who has been pulling the strings since this whole thing started? Who has been stringing us along this whole time? Who made Taurus give us the warehouse? Who promised both Taurus and us the Sunsphere?"

"The mayor." Emma's voice was full of doubt as she wondered where Free was going with this.

"Big Joe. A puppet master if ever I saw one. I think we've been his deluded little puppets this whole time. He's just been moving us around like pawns on a chessboard."

"I don't know, Free. David always talked about how Mayor Early was a master manipulator, but he never mentioned anything illegal."

"Think about it, Emma!" Free was becoming much more animated. "You worry that David was on the take. What if Big Joe was *making* him take those bribes? You said yourself it was so unlike David. I hate to say it, but what if the mayor is *making* Taurus move these canisters? He has international connections. Taurus is just a big fish in a small pond."

"I think that's a lot of what ifs, especially on the word of a tarot card reading."

"A tarot card reading that's true. It predicted death. Pearly's dead. It predicted conflict with a businessman. Taurus. And it predicted a Puppet Master behind the scenes. I think that's the mayor."

They were in Farragut Township now. The truck signaled a right turn at the high school. They stopped to watch it disappear behind the main building.

"What's back there?" Emma asked.

"Woods? I don't know. Let's backtrack to the road behind the school. We'll sneak up on them from behind."

They parked the car a good distance from the truck and watched as the two men transferred the contents of the truck to the back of a paneled van. Attached to the van was a commercial riding mower on a trailer. Two more men who looked like lawn care technicians assisted them. Emma took more pictures.

"I can't see the plates. I'm sneaking closer," Free said.

Emma laid a hand on his arm. "Free, no. It's too dangerous."

"I've got to, Emma. We can't see anything from here. Take the keys. Scoot over here and be ready to drive away when I get back. Pull out your phone. If anything goes down, call your detective buddy."

She watched him disappear into the foliage.

***

Free bent down low as he made his way through the shrubs behind the school. As he drew closer, he watched as the Big R driver got a signature from one of the van drivers.

"Yeah, thanks for coming out. We just finished mowing here and live farther west, so this was very helpful," one of them said.

"No problem, man. It's our job," said the Big R driver.

As the Big R truck ambled off the way it had come, the two men looked at each other and smirked. "What a bunch of rubes in this town." They both laughed as they ducked into the back of the van to secure their cargo.

Free couldn't see the license plate because the trailer was in the way. He crept closer for a better view. From within the van he heard one say, "I told him that damned Sunsphere was no good. We would have been made that first night if you hadn't taken care of that girl."

"He's an idiot, but you can't beat the money. Tighten that one down and we're out of here."

Free had to hurry. He inched closer to the trailer for a better view of the plate. No good. He scurried across the parking lot, keeping low until he was directly behind the trailer. He sat for a minute catching his breath with his back to the hitch. Listening for sounds from the van, he peeked around it and found himself nose to kneecap with one of the deliverymen. That was when everything went black.

***

Emma held her breath as she watched Free sidle up to the back of the trailer. The two men had disappeared inside, presumably securing the load. Why wasn't there a license plate on the trailer? It seemed stupid to be in violation of such a simple law while hauling illegal goods.

Free sat with his back to the trailer for just a minute. What was he doing? He can't take on those guys alone. Emma stifled a scream as she watched one of the men, a tall, burly redhead, emerge from the truck and move in Free's direction. When Free finally pulled himself up to look around, the redhead was there with a tire tool he'd pulled quietly from the back of the trailer.

The blow had been swift and hard. Oh god. Was he alive? She sat in shock as they dragged him to the back of the van. Hands shaking, Emma started the truck and pulled it down to the end of the driveway and across the street to the Gas N Go. She could follow the van from there. Once parked, she fumbled with her phone and Detective Green's card.

"This is Detective Andrew Green. I'm away at other business right now, but if you'll leave a message at the tone, I'll get back to you."

"Yes, this is Emma Goode. I need your help. I'm ready to tell you everything. I'm following a van with stolen tanks from Oak Ridge. These are the guys Tiffany Sims was following when she died. We think they are the murderers. They've kidnapped Free Byrd. He's unconscious in the back. I'm trying to get you a license plate number. I'm heading west out of Farragut." She dropped her phone back in her pocket and put the truck in gear as the van crawled onto the main road. She was right behind them.

***

"Goddammit goddammit goddammit!"

When Free came to, one of his captors was beating his head against the dash. The sight made his pounding head hurt even more. What had they hit him with?

"For the love of God, Red! Will you stop that, you crazy fucker?"

"This job has been a goddamned train wreck from the beginning. What the hell is wrong with these people, Dex? And what are we going to do with that one?"

"I don't know yet. I'm thinking."

Free slowly tried to move his hands and feet, with no luck. He was sitting upright with his hands duct taped behind him around the bottom of a shelf. The Y-12 tanks clanked as the van drove on the uneven pavement. He kept his head down so his captors wouldn't know he was awake. The duct tape on his mouth pulled at his stubble.

"Okay. I got it. We drop the van at the motel and take this asshole back to the Sunsphere. We'll lock him in at the top and let the Boss take care of him. It's not our problem. We did our job. We don't need another murder."

"Damn straight, we don't need another murder," Red muttered. "But this plan don't sound good. The more we loiter around that damned Sunsphere, the closer we come to being caught."

"Well, what do you want to do? What's your big plan, Mr. Just-Kill-Her-and-Run? You're damned lucky this one found her before the police. They're not even looking for you."

"Exactly the reason we need to get the hell out of here. I say we just leave him in the motel room with these cans. Then they can get him for murder *and* terrorism."

Dex reached over and slapped Red on the head. "You know why that's a bad idea, Einstein? We're in this up to our necks. If we don't deliver, our asses get handed to us—our very dead asses."

"We should have just gotten out of here when we picked them up instead of all this waiting around."

"And take them where? We had to pull them out of the reservation when the opportunity presented itself. Is it our fault that stupid boss wanted them stored in the most visible landmark in town? Jeez, what an idiot."

"Well, we can't leave the canisters at the motel unguarded. That's stupid."

"So I'll stay with them. I'll call the boss's man and have him meet you at the Sunsphere. Hand this guy off and head back. Then we'll be on our way. I made contact with that foreign professor at the festival. He told me where to take this shit. Then we're done."

"Finally. God, it's like a puzzle. I wish someone had just told us where to go from the start."

"Well, that would have been logical, wouldn't it? Plus, the big guys can claim ignorance of the bigger plan if they get caught. Ever think it's us that'll go down big time for all of it if *we* get caught? This whole scheme was fucked from the start."

"What is it, anyway?" Red looked back at the canisters curiously.

"I dunno. Could be radioactive for all we know."

"Can't be radioactive, dipshit. We would have poisoning by now."

Free's head rolled on his shoulders and he was out—again.

Dex and Red pulled into a rundown drive-in motel far west of Knoxville. Dex drove past the small office with its '50s style neon sign, straight to a seedy cottage at the back of the property. He pulled the van behind the building and jumped out. Red crawled over his seat and squatted down to cut the tape from around Free's wrists. Free moaned, but was still unconscious.

Dex uncoupled the trailer from the van and opened the back. Together they dragged Free out and put him in the passenger side of an old green Mazda.

"Tape him in good. I don't want him coming to and clocking me," Red said.

***

Emma sat with the truck idling outside the motel wondering what her next move should be. Finally, she drove slowly down the driveway past the office. Just a few cottages shy of the end, she pulled in front of one of the units and started out on foot in the direction she saw the van go. Fortunately, the tree-lined parking lot afforded her some cover. The cottages, about ten in all, faced the driveway. She carefully picked her way around the back buildings until she found the van. She peered around the bungalow and watched them load Free into another car.

The license plate of the van was finally unobstructed. Pulling the pen and the card out of her pocket, she wrote it down and headed back for the truck.

Once again, she angled the truck on the road, this time pointing toward home. She took a phone picture of the blinking motel sign, Mountain Rest Motel. She guessed the kidnappers were heading back to Knoxville.

It was a lucky guess. When the green Mazda came barreling out of the motel, she moved out onto the highway. She dialed Detective Green again and left the license plate numbers in his message box. She dropped her phone beside her as she concentrated on keeping up and staying back.

Less than an hour later, Emma was surprised to see the Mazda pulling back into the World's Fair Plaza. She threw the truck in park at the entrance to the parking garage and, tossing the keys to the parking attendant, ran ahead on foot. She shot down the stairs to the Sunsphere just in time to see the car backing up to the ground level service entrance. The door opened and the car backed in.

***

Free woke up on his back in a concrete hole with the early evening sky overhead. As his senses slowly returned, he found his hands were once again taped—this time in front—as were his feet and knees. He brought his taped hands up to shield his eyes from the sun, then gently removed the tape on his mouth. He squinted as he looked around in shock. He struggled until he was upright and realized, to his disbelief, that he was sitting outside at the very top of the Sunsphere. The concrete, donut-shaped crater was just wide enough to walk around. That hatch on the ground must be the way down.

He furiously worked to free himself. Maybe he could get down those stairs and get help. His head spun as he twisted to reach the silver tape at his knees and began tearing at it bit by bit.

***

It took some doing, but Free finally ripped the last of the tape off his hands. He stumbled to the hatch but found it locked up tight. Looking over the edge of the structure, he shouted and waved to the crowd below. A few people looked up and waved back. That's when he noticed the thick puddles of rope around two metal hooks along the short wall. They were connected to both sides of some sort of sign. Thank God someone had hung a banner across the front of the Sunsphere. He picked up one of the ropes and wrapped the end around his hands. He looked over the edge again. No way could he rappel down the side. His best bet might be to jump the lip and hide there until help arrived. No, he would just have to wait here and fight it out when they came back for him. Before he could look around for something to use as a weapon, he heard the creak of the hatch opening.

Red and Jerod Warner climbed up into the enclosure. Red had a rifle, which he immediately pointed at Free.

"Hold still, partner," he said menacingly. "What are you going to do? Jump?"

Jerod laughed as Red raised his rifle. Then, "Whoa, what are you standing in, Red?"

Red looked down quickly at his feet and noticed he was standing on a large tuft of what looked like black hair.

"A wig? I don't know. Shut up."

"Wigs? I thought that was just a joke."

Red kicked it with his foot, eyes still trained on Free.

"Spider nest!" Jerod let out a high-pitched squeal and headed toward the ladder. Red looked down to see a black swarm of spiders crawling lightning fast up his leg, so many that his leg had nearly disappeared.

"Get 'em off! Get 'em off!" Red's gun clattered to the floor as he leapt and batted at his pants. The gun fired. Jerod went down screaming.

"My foot! You shot my foot!"

Seeing no alternative, Free held tight to his rope and vaulted over the edge.

« CHAPTER 14 »

EMMA PATTED HER POCKETS frantically for her phone, then remembered she'd dropped it in the truck. She searched the crowd around her for security or even someone with a cell phone. That's when she heard the announcer on the loudspeaker.

"Ladies and gentlemen, thank you for being here tonight. Here to announce his new Green Initiative is our illustrious city administrator Mayor Joe Early. Let's give him a big welcome."

The crowd cheered. A few boos sifted over the speaker. Emma ran in that direction.

The open-air amphitheater was a stage set before rising concrete bleachers. Massive white tent-like structures formed its roof. The bleachers faced the Sunsphere, upon which hung a gigantic banner reading "Growing Green." It sported a logo of the Sunsphere with a leaf growing out of its base and the words "Support Knoxville's Green Initiative." As

Emma ran for the podium erected onstage for the event, she saw the mayor had already stepped up.

"Hello Knoxvillians! We are here tonight to discuss a very exciting plan for our city."

She ran past the crew and headed for the stage. She charged straight for the microphone. Mayor Early, startled, stuttered, "Ms. Goode! Please be seated."

Emma looked frantically around until she spied Jackson Taurus. She pushed the mayor out of the way.

"I need help. My friend and colleague Free Byrd has been kidnapped by Tiffany Sims' murderers. They've taken him to the Sunsphere."

"Security!" The mayor motioned the uniformed men forward.

Emma pointed to Taurus. "This man, Jackson Taurus, is behind a plot to smuggle contraband from Y-12 to unknown buyers. His helpers are the ones who are holding Free."

The crowd gasped. Security ran on stage to hustle Emma off. "Taurus. Get Taurus," Emma yelled. As she swatted away the uniformed men, Taurus jumped from his chair.

"That's a bold allegation, Ms. Goode. Where's your proof?"

"Right here. I have a picture of your cronies taking the cylinders to the Sunsphere to a floor that can only be accessed by you."

Rowdy and Orville sprang at Taurus from the front row bleacher. One on each arm, they held him fast at the dais.

"I demand a lawyer," he yelled. "Unhand me."

Morticia ran up to the stage, ripped the lid off her vial, and threw her herbal concoction at the dais.

Taurus sneezed. His outrage turned to confusion as he stopped fighting his attackers and spoke into the microphone. "It's the mayor. He's blackmailing me."

"He's telling the truth," Morticia called from the sidelines.

All eyes turned to the mayor. The blood drained from Mayor Early's face. He looked around at the frightening crowd, growing louder and more crazed by the second. The tightly wound coil of recent tensions was ready to spring.

He turned and ran.

"He's getting away!" screamed Rowdy.

The crowd went berserk. A gunshot rang out from the direction of the Sunsphere.

"Look on the Sunsphere!" Al's shrill voice rose above the mayhem. "Some guy is hanging on it."

Now their attention snapped to the gleaming, golden landmark. Someone was indeed suspended in front of the sign. Two men stood at the top. One had a rifle.

"He's got a gun!"

True to their Tennessee Volunteer nickname, the audience didn't stand and gape. They had been primed for weeks for this press conference and were ready to take action. Rowdy and Orville pushed Taurus out of the way as they scrambled off the stage toward the shining globe. They surged as one toward the Sunsphere with God's Warriors in the lead. Security personnel released Emma and ran through the crowd after them. By the time the Warriors stood at the elevator at the base of the structure, their concealed carry weapons were drawn. With a nod from Rowdy, they stormed the Sunsphere.

***

Against the dusky skyline, Emma could make out figures struggling atop the building. The crowd screamed and most hit the plaza when gunshots were fired from above. Free was still dangling precariously, smacking repeatedly against the Growing Green sign. More screams escaped the crowd as he lost his grip and slid further down the rope. Legions of police had mobilized around the structure, pushing onlookers back in an attempt to secure the area. Emma skirted around their sawhorses and ran for the stairs before the barrier was completely in place.

Throwing off her pumps, she ran up the stairs as fast she could against the tide of people streaming back down.

"Fuck that, I ain't getting shot," a voice carried over the crowd.

At the fourth floor—familiar territory—she headed for the elevator. Once inside, she pressed the eighth-floor button. Locked. She headed for the stairs.

At the top was madness. Rowdy had his arm around Red's neck, dragging him down the ladder from the outside into the stairwell. Men stood holding the eighth-floor door open with pistols trained on Red, yelling for him to stand down. Jerod fought like a wounded animal until he got the butt of a pistol to the head. He dropped like a sack of potatoes. All were screaming.

"Free! Somebody get Free up!" Emma yelled.

Two men holstered their guns, helped Rowdy pull Red through the doors, and stormed up the stairs. Emma followed.

***

Free's rope was longer than he thought. He sailed right past the top two panes of the orb, losing any chance of a foothold. He slammed hard into the building when the rope went taut, his grip slipping. His head throbbed as he hugged the rope desperately. He wasn't sure how much longer he could hang on. Blood dripping from his raw hands slickened the rope and threatened his already precarious grip.

"Help! Help! Please, somebody!"

Minutes passed as he waited for help that might never come.

"Well, Pearly, looks like we'll be united soon," he whispered.

He felt an upward pull, and nearly lost his grip again when a rush of relief flooded him. Slowly the rope inched upward. He half-limped, half-walked the final feet to the top.

Two pairs of hands hoisted him over. Emma ran forward, helping him to the ground.

"Oh, God. Free. Are you okay?" She looked him over carefully.

"My head is killing me, but I think I'll live," he said, slumping. "The canisters. They're at a motel."

"I know. I followed you there. I got a license plate number."

"We've got to tell the police."

"I sent it all to Green's voicemail. I hope he got it."

"Let's get you out of here." Orville stepped up to help Free to his feet. Together the two men and Emma piloted him down the ladder and to the elevator.

***

Detective Green was preparing a team to enter the Sunsphere when Emma, Free, and Orville stepped out at ground level.

"Those vigilantes have them under control," Emma said. "You just need to send somebody in to make the arrests."

Green nodded to an officer beside him, who left with two others to do just that.

"I got your messages. We've sent a team to the motel to check it out. Thanks, but you do realize you should have called me first before putting yourself in danger like that."

"I tried," Emma said. "You should answer your phone."

He gave her that crooked smile again before turning to Free. "You need medical help. Hang on." He motioned for an EMT.

Free let go of Orville and stepped closer to Green. "The one upstairs. Red. He is the one who killed Pearly. I overheard them talking. They are getting ready to deliver the canisters to their buyer. They got detained here in town because their rendezvous plans got screwed up. Apparently their contact was one of the speakers at the International Fair. I don't know who."

"You were right, Free," Emma said. "Taurus indicted the mayor when I outed him. The mayor was our Puppet Master."

"Where is the Mayor?" Free looked around at the people jostling the police barriers.

As they peered into the crowd, a figure raced toward them. The mayor ran full throttle with Spyder in hot pursuit. The Reverend huffed along, bringing up the rear. Mayor Early jagged to the left, while Spyder charged straight at him for the tackle. They both went down, arse over elbows, and landed in a heap on the concrete. The Reverend pulled up beside them as the crowd scattered. He grabbed the mayor's hands with one meaty hand while he unfastened his suspenders with the other. Spyder pulled off his cloth belt while he held tight to the mayor's feet. Their hands worked at lightning speed and they both jumped back at the same time.

The crowd applauded as Spyder and the Reverend proudly stood over a hog-tied mayor.

"Where'd you learn to tie knots like that?" the Reverend asked.

"Junior rodeo," Spyder answered. "You?"

"Church camp."

The two beamed at one another as the mayor squirmed.

***

The next morning Leonard Sheldon's front page article in the *Spotlight* broke the story before anyone else in town. Every news outlet picked it up, including the national wire service.

Mayor, Knoxville Businessman at Center of Nuclear Trafficking Plot

KNOXVILLE, Tenn.-- Knoxville Mayor Joseph Early was arrested last night for an alleged corruption conspiracy involving nuclear-related materials trafficking and campaign fraud to fund his campaign for senator.

Federal agents arrested Early at a Green Initiative press conference at the World's Fair Plaza. He was driven to the federal courthouse while his offices in Knoxville were raided. His office has been under surveillance since January for campaign fraud, authorities say.

The charges against Early include trafficking in nuclear-related materials that could be used to make weapons of mass destruction, eight counts of a scheme to defraud citizens of his services, and wire fraud. More charges including blackmail and extortion could follow, say city officials. A hand-cuffed and shackled Early was remanded into custody pending a bail hearing later this week.

Also arrested was area businessman Jackson Taurus, president and CEO of Taurus Enterprises. According to arrest records, he is charged with illegally obtaining and transporting materials between June 17 and June 24 that "could contribute to the design, development, manufacture, deployment, use, or maintenance of weapons of mass destruction." While being led away, he told reporters he was being blackmailed by the mayor. An investigation is underway.

Mayoral Assistant Jerod Warner has been detained for questioning for his involvement in the conspiracy and trafficking schemes. Charges are pending, says Detective Andrew Green, arresting officer.

Two other men were arrested for possession of nuclear-related materials with intent to resale and transport across state lines. Dexter Summers and Michael "Red" Campbell have ties to New York mob boss "Fat Eddy" Adamo. Campbell also is a suspect in the murder of Tiffany Sims, found dead at the World's Fair Park on June 17 (see related story). Authorities allege that she came upon the two men as they were transporting and storing the contraband above Taurus' office in the Sunsphere.

Y-12 officials say the contents of the 30 canisters found in possession of Summers and Campbell is classified, but the materials are not radioactive. The tanks have been returned to the HEUM facility. The nuclear reservation has been under fire of late for lax security. A Department of Energy spokesperson says inquiries are pending. A team of nuclear inspectors have been on the scene at the World's Fair Park since the arrests.

***

Arrest Made in Death of Political Activist

KNOXVILLE, Tenn.--An arrest has been made in the murder of Tiffany Sims, the political activist who was killed in the early hours of June 17 beneath the Sunsphere. The 22-year-old was found badly beaten and drowned in the lake at the World's Fair Plaza.

Michael "Red" Campbell, a career criminal with mob ties, has been charged with the murder. In a stunning development, he confessed to the murder shortly after his arrest on June 24. DNA testing has linked him to the crime.

Campbell and a partner, Dexter Summers, both of New York City, allegedly were transporting stolen canisters from Oak Ridge's Y-12 reservation to the Sunsphere when they encountered Sims at the scene.

The Y-12 theft is at the heart of the current charges against Knoxville Mayor Joe Early, who allegedly masterminded the plot to sell the materials to an unknown source for campaign funds.

Sims had been on a kNOxNUKES mission to track vehicles going to and from Y-12, according to a NukeWatcher spokesperson. kNOxNUKES is the local chapter of the national nuclear watchdog organization. She was not on an officially sanctioned mission, but her team did call in twice to the national clearinghouse, said Zane Bozman of NukeWatcher.

"We know that she was with Alcinda Jakes and Manfred Watson, two at-large members of our organization," he said. "We received license plate numbers of suspicious vehicles leaving Y-12, which we have given to your local law enforcement. The three also requested we activate our nationwide tracker teams to follow the suspicious vehicles across state lines, but we didn't receive the message in time."

Bozman further states that Jakes and Watson have not contacted NukeWatcher since the calls, nor have they been located by law enforcement.

"They travel the country and are often off the grid," Bozman said.

Free Byrd, Sims' boyfriend, was arrested at the scene of the crime. He was later released. Sims left a phone message that she was in trouble before her murder, he said. She asked him to meet her at the Amphitheater.

"She told me something suspicious was going on at the Sunsphere. She had tracked some trucks from Y-12 and was watching them haul them into the tower. When I got there, she was dead."

« CHAPTER 15 »

VERGIE AND THE REVEREND SAT at Vergie's patio table with the *Press* opened between them.

"I still can't believe the Mayor was into all them illegal doings," the Reverend said. "I knew the man. He seemed God-fearing."

"Well, you never know, Reverend. They can pull the wool over your eyes sometimes."

"Did you know that Night Crow and Spyder asked me to officiate at their legal wedding next month? They're having some kind of wedding festival first. A handfast? Something like that."

Vergie tsked. "They are some very strange people."

"True, but remember Ephesians 4, Vergie. *I urge you to walk in a manner worthy of the calling to which you have been called, with all humility and gentleness, with patience, bearing with one another in love, eager to maintain the unity of the Spirit in the bond of peace.*

Vergie eyed him doubtfully.

"You catch more flies with honey than with vinegar, Vergie. If we welcome them and stand in the Lord, we'll win them over one day."

"Yes, but you're awful buddy buddy with them all of a sudden."

"That Spyder and I kind of bonded when we took down the mayor. He's a man same as me, just thinks different. We'll bring him around."

Vergie looked back down at the paper. "Says here the green plan is still intact even if the mayor *is* gone. I think his deputy mayor put it all together anyway, and she's in charge now. She probably ran the city anyway. Sounds like he was too busy breaking laws."

"I know some conservative politicians and businessmen who are glad the Mayor got his. There have always been rumors about his backdoor deals. We must pray for them all, Vergie."

"Yes, Reverend. We must. And for that poor girl who was murdered. She was a sinner, but I don't want to see anybody dead."

"Amen, Sister Vergie. So, have you made peace with your neighbors?"

"I haven't actually apologized, but I've forgiven them in my heart. They lost their way, I know. But they did some good work with that whole murder investigating thing."

The Reverend smiled fondly at her. "I'm proud of you. We've all come a long way."

"Except for Rowdy," Vergie said. "How is he now?"

"I was awful proud of him when he took down that murderer. As soon as they hauled that guy off to jail, Rowdy came down with some kind of pox. He was itching something awful. The ambulance took him to the hospital. I visited yesterday. He's getting better."

"What was wrong with him?"

"They never figured it out. Some kind of severe dermatitis. They think he might have come in contact with some kind of irritant? They're holding him for a few days to be sure he didn't contract some kind of radiation poisoning or something."

"The Oak Ridge people say that stuff wasn't radioactive, Reverend."

"I don't believe a word they say. If that's the case, why are there men in white suits with Geiger counters all over the World's Fair? They ain't even saying what it was."

"Poor Rowdy. I bet he's not happy you've come to terms with the pagans."

"Not so much, but he'll come around, too."

***

One door down, Emma and Free also sat on the patio drinking coffee and soaking up the morning sun.

"Have you talked to Abe and Edward? This stuff has been all over the national news." A banged-up Free attempted to hold his coffee cup with two bandaged hands. One arm was in a sling. He had a cast on the opposite leg.

"Yes," Emma sighed. "They both got packages from Taurus and they both destroyed them. I feel so relieved. You were right about telling them. I think they did much better with it than me."

"In my experience, honesty is always best. Plus, they had a very supportive mother at their side to help them through it. You did good, Em."

Emma patted Free's good leg. "I couldn't have done it without you, friend. Do you need a straw?"

"No, I'll manage."

"The pagans are holding a memorial for Pearly this weekend. Think you'll be able to go?"

"Yes, if I have to crawl. I may need some help."

"Not a problem." Emma opened her laptop and brought up the newspaper website. News of the mayor and his mob ties, as well as Y-12 security had been dominating the front page for days. "Says here Interim Mayor Wanda Hopper is expected to run for mayor in the special election."

"She's got my vote," Free said.

"Mine too. Say, we got some mail while we were so busy this week."

"Busy? Is that what we're calling it?"

"We got our 501(c)(3) status—KUE is now a nonprofit. Plus we got our official grant award, so we don't have to worry about the mayor's problems in relation to it. I think Wanda would have pushed it through for us, but it's a load off nonetheless."

"Man, that's great news. We've got a lot to do."

"Yes, we do. Also, I know you like your teepee, but I want you to have your own room in the house. How about room and board in exchange for presiding over the nonprofit? I think you should be president of KUE, Free. You've been the driving force behind our progress. I think you deserve it."

Free gave Emma his first smile in days. "President Free. I like the sound of that. We'll have to get ourselves a volunteer army together to keep things going while I heal."

"We'll get it done. I've been getting a lot of calls from your friends on Market Square. They're worrying about the warehouse and have offered to help keep it going. I have some contact numbers here. Maybe you can make some calls while you laze around." It was Emma's turn to smile.

"What a relief. I've been worrying about pulling things together."

"And, of course, I cleaned out your yard cart so I could pull you around the yard and get your expert advice on what needs to be done here."

This time Free laughed. "I don't think you need that kind of micromanagement, Emma. But I'm happy to offer you advice should you need it. Besides, I'll be on my feet soon."

They sat in silence and looked over the backyard. The chickens were clucking peacefully. Bees were buzzing around the hydrangeas. The miniature goats played king of the mountain on a metal tub in their lot. The garden was bursting out around them in an explosion of lush green color.

"I'll do your critter duty if you do press interviews," Emma said.

"Deal. I'll assign warehouse shifts if you weed the tomatoes."

"Deal. You've got to get off your butt and get that Sunsphere project off the ground. I hear the lease is available late next month."

"I'll do it in exchange for help with the next two weeks' vegetable harvest."

The bartering was flying around so fast and furious that Emma wasn't sure who owed what to whom, but if anyone could keep track of it all, it was her and Free.

KNOXTOPIA
Plant a Garden. Change the World.

As I two-finger type this blog entry, I am so very grateful for good, honest friends. All is well on the farmstead. Emma and I were marveling just the other day at how things have been thriving and growing without a lot of help from us. We feed the animals, weed a bit, and enjoy the fruits of our labor. The farm is giving us a brief respite while I heal, but before long (very soon, in fact) we will be working our butts off harvesting and putting food by. Then there's the little issue of greening the house.

We've put together a gang of volunteers and several interns to keep the warehouse going. I'm finally off bed rest and able to at least hobble down to supervise. We're already harvesting hydroponic greens for our restaurants. Head downtown for KUE Gardens salad greens and herbs! Participating restaurants have put signs in their windows, plus we have listed them on this website's sidebar. Check it out. Soon we'll have much, much more to offer.

We are taking applications for nonprofit organizations and sustainable businesses for our Sunsphere project. I wanted to spearhead this, but I just can't do it all. Hey, you solar businesses, we would love to offer you some space within our organization. If you haven't already heard from us, give us a call. We haven't taken possession of the building yet—that's weeks away—but we are trying to get our ducks in a row.

I've mentioned before how excited I am by the green explosion in our community. KUE is working closely with the acting mayor to further the goals of the Green Initiative. Emma and I are heading up the City Farm Initiative and need your input. Contact me for committee times and come on down to help us brainstorm.

I would be remiss if I didn't mention the beautiful spirit of cooperation that has descended upon our community. We've been through a lot this spring, haven't we? With the disruption of local government and the amazing leadership of our interim mayor, it feels like we've made a fresh start. Sure, there have been a few bumps in the road, but things are much, much better, aren't they? The protests downtown have stopped. Talk radio has calmed down. Life is good.

Speaking of talk radio, congratulations to Leonard Sheldon and his new radio show on 1310 AM. *Civil Discourse* will feature sensible discussions with the Left and Right about how we can come together and move forward as a city.

Knoxville, you've renewed my faith in the human race. Together we're going to build a great city.

5,016 Comments

TOP COMMENTS

Radio_Al said ...

I hope you don't think this is over. The revolution has just begun.

(555 Comments View)

TheReverend said ...

Our prayers have been answered for a peaceful resolution to this troubling problem. We will continue to pray for our town and every single member, no matter their race, creed, religion, or sexual or political preference.

(199 Comments View)

XXXAnnieSpeaksXXX said ...

Great post. Comment back at AnnieSpeaks, a blog for and about Knoxville night life!

(69 comments <u>View</u>)

<u>VIEW ALL COMMENTS</u>

« EPILOGUE »

IT WAS JUST BEFORE DAWN when a figure crouched among the low shrubbery in front of the downtown Knoxville tunnel. Al Scheeder opened his backpack and pulled out several cans of spray paint. He was sorry it had come to this, but he needed to boost the signal. He wasn't quite sure what had happened to his radio setup, but he hadn't been able to broadcast since his first great episode of *Pirate Al in the Morning*. He planned to climb up the fire escape of the Grow House when he was finished here.

Al was particularly proud of this plan of his. He was going to paint a message on the precious tunnel for all to see just in time for the morning commute. The white face of the tunnel, now graying from exhaust and air pollution, was the perfect canvas. He had no idea how the city had kept it so pristine for so long, especially since there were so many excellent taggers in town. He guessed he needed a tag name.

The good names like Uneak and Skram were already taken. Maybe Trūf? You know, because he spoke Truth.

He shook the can of red paint and set to work. After a while he traded it for the black can. He giggled as he wrote, stopping often to vigorously shake the can between sprays.

The single whoop of a police siren froze him in his tracks.

"Drop the can and show me your hands," a voice boomed over the megaphone.

Al dropped the can mid-sentence and turned slowly around, hands held high. Two policemen approached with guns drawn.

"What kind of idiot tags the Knoxville tunnel, Burns?"

"A big idiot, Caswell. One who doesn't realize he's being recorded on a traffic cam the whole time."

"Shit," Al said.

"One who doesn't realize that the City of Knoxville really, really hates tunnel taggers, Burns."

"Let's take him for a little ride, Caswell."

Hand-cuffed and thrown in the back of the car, Al was escorted to the jailhouse.

If Al thought he had gotten away with property theft at 1310 AM Talk Radio, he quickly discovered that he had not. The station managers had not only reported the theft but given police surveillance tape evidence of the crime. As a result, a warrant had been issued for his arrest. FCC charges were also pending for his station hijack. The managers had happily handed over audio tapes of Pirate Al as well. While the FCC usually doesn't arrest for piracy on the first offence, they were apparently urged to do so by one Representative Darrell Andaryl. Al tried to lessen his sentence by telling them where the "borrowed" equipment could be found, but all that got him was an additional charge of trespassing.

Later that morning, commuters were slowed down by a city crew parked at the tunnel entrance. Drivers who got there early enough were treated to a large red outline of an elephant. Inside the elephant dripping in black were the words "Kiss my American ass."

"Somebody really hates circuses," said a crewman.

"Damned vegan hippies," said his partner.

Read an excerpt from
Book 2 of the Urban Farm Mystery series:

FREE RANGE MURDER

« Preface »

THE MAN IN BLACK HIKED through the woods to avoid detection, sliding through the trees like a shadow. The half moon illuminated his path just enough so that he could find his way without a light. He gripped the tactical flashlight anyway, thinking he might need it soon enough to see—or to defend himself. He slipped out of the woods and pressed his back against the end of the long barn. Holding the flashlight between his legs, he pulled a small night vision camcorder out of his deep vest pocket. He checked to make sure it was ready to record and pulled his black bandana high up over his nose—more to keep the smell at bay than for camouflage. The ammonia from the chicken operation made his eyes water. The smell of decay assaulted his nose.

He trained the camera on two trucks around the corner of the barn. The vehicles were running with headlights pointed at the door. Six men worked in the dead of night slinging dead and sick chickens into garbage pails. They held the chickens by the hocks, two or three in each gloved hand. If conscious birds fought for freedom, the men slammed them hard against the barn siding. They alternately cursed at the birds and laughed at each other.

After a few minutes he turned off the camera and pocketed it. He had identified all the entrances on an earlier reconnaissance trip so he knew his way around. He hugged the building as he made his way around to a side door and slipped in undetected. The lights were on inside. Hoping to conserve the batteries on the camcorder, he pulled out his phone and started recording.

"I've just entered the third chicken barn at Clucks-A-Lot Egg Farm," he spoke softly into the phone's microphone. "As you can see, conditions here are deplorable. I estimate there are at least 50,000 chickens in this barn. The smell is unbearable. I'll let the video speak for itself."

He moved stealthily down the corridor, recording the battery cages full of wall-to-wall birds—six or eight in each. The cages were stacked seven tiers high and extended the length of the barn. He zoomed in on trampled chickens inside cages and the ones caught in the wires at odd angles, unable to get free. Their cage mates viciously pecked them with clipped beaks.

He walked back the way he had come and stepped into the night. He paused for the time it took to send the phone video to his colleague. That should be enough footage to indict this operation, he thought. The night vision footage will strengthen the case.

He pulled the camcorder out again to record the workers. Dragging their full pails, they crossed the yard to a series of covered pits. As they threw open the lids, one of the workers yelled, "Time to make the chicken soup!" They all laughed and hooted as they dumped the dead and injured fowl into the pits. When they were done, they cleared away the containers and cages, and loaded themselves into the trucks, three abreast. Engines knocking and radios humming, they ambled down the rutted road toward the highway.

The man in black stood against the barn until all he could hear were the sounds of frantic chickens and tree frogs. He cautiously made his way to the pits and lifted a lid. Turning on his flashlight, he was shocked to see signs of life within the mound of decaying chicken carcasses. As he turned on the camcorder to record the horror, a hard blow to the back of his head knocked him into the deep pit. The lid slammed down hard with a metallic clank.

Look for this title late summer 2014.

Subscribe to Yvonne Loveday's Newsletter at

http://yvonneloveday.com/newsletter/

for up-to-date information on upcoming books.

Acknowledgements

To Granny, Mom, and the rest of the tribe

This book would not have been possible without the love and support of my family. I know, every author says that. I guess because it's true. However, I really put these people through their paces. It would take another book to recount the many ways they have made my life better and writing easier. I am extremely blessed to come from a family of readers.

Many thanks to my beta readers: Solomon Bryant, Tovah Greenwood, Mamie Lee Loveday, Robert Loveday, and Leigh Evans Loveday. I am especially grateful to Solomon, who must have been an author in another life. Many times he helped me throw words at the wall to see what stuck and listened to my writing conundrums. His advice was sound, more often than not. Family, thanks for having faith in my ability. It meant the world to me.

To my grandsons: I want to thank Isaiah Bryant for amusing himself so often while I wrote. I'm sure it was sometimes boring for him. The idea for this book was formed shortly after Yuma Livesay was born. I held him as a newborn while these ideas percolated in my head. Both these amazing young men are a constant inspiration to me.

Author Carolyn Jourdan was a lifesaver and a cheerleader during the writing and publishing process. I couldn't have done it without her. I know I drove her crazy at times with all the instant messaging. She is a good soul. Read her books. They are wonderful.

Ben Epperson is my cover model. I'm sure he's the reason you picked up this book. Thanks to Cruze Farm in Knoxville, Tennessee, for letting us roam around and take pictures. Photographer Tovah Greenwood was indispensable in creating the visual aspects of this project. She is the most gracious, lovely lady I know. Please see her incredible work at www.tovahlovephotography.com.

And finally, I want to thank my two oldest sons, Joseph and Levi Greenwood. I'm so proud of all you've accomplished. You are never far from my thoughts. I love you both!

About the Author

Yvonne Loveday was born and raised in Knoxville, Tennessee. She broke out and ran around the country for a decade, but eventually came back. She got a degree in journalism and wrote for local newspapers before settling into public relations for a good, long time. She broke out of that, too.

Her love of all things green began as a youngster when her grandmother let her borrow *Organic Gardening and Farming* magazines. Together they read regional authors. Granny often said the Good Old Days weren't that good. Yvonne never really believed her. She also said Yvonne should be a writer. Yvonne is just now thinking that might be a possibility.

Live Green or Die Trying is her first work of fiction. When Yvonne isn't writing, she's obsessively knitting, watching cult TV, or reading. She lives with her son, grandson, three black cats, and a dachshund named Mr. Magoo. She really can't explain her obsession with the Sunsphere.

Connect with Me Online

On the Web:
http://www.yvonneloveday.com

Facebook:
Yvonne Loveday Author

Twitter:
@yvonneloveday

Pinterest:

http://www.pinterest.com/knoxtopia/